Lies, Betrayals,

Fear

Faces Behind the Stones 3

By

Fran Lewis

World Castle Publishing, LLC

This is a work of fiction. Names, characters, places, and incidents are products of the author's imagination or are used fictitiously and are not to be construed as real. Any resemblance to actual events, locations, organizations, or person, living or dead, is entirely coincidental.

WCP

World Castle Publishing, LLC
Pensacola, Florida

Copyright © Fran Lewis 2013
ISBN: 9781939865984
First Edition World Castle Publishing, LLC October 1, 2013
http://www.worldcastlepublishing.com

Cover: Karen Fuller
Photos: Shutterstock
Editor: Maxine Bringenberg

DEDICATION

This third book in the series is quite unique and special. There are many people who have supported me in all of my endeavors. This past February I lost my best friend. Her name was Florence Monacelli. We taught at the same school for over 20 years and when she passed away not only was I surprised that she died but also I knew she is someone that could never be replaced. Always there for everyone no matter how ill she was or what she had to do. Florence was the one person who always had the right answers, found the time to help guide you through a serious problem to a solution and thought that being an author was cool. Learning that I did radio really gave her a jolt as she listened to my shows and often provided great suggestions for how I could improve them. She was the older sister I never had and was there when my sister passed away to fill a serious void in my heart. I dedicate this book to her memory and our everlasting friendship. Florence passed away on Monday, February 25, 2013.

ACKNOWLEDGEMENTS

A special thank you to my wonderful editor Maxine Bringenberg for keeping me centered and on task. To those who volunteered to become part of my stories and allowed themselves to be behind a stone I would like to thank Karen Vaughan and Ashley Fontainne two outstanding writers, authors and reviewers. To my sister Marcia Joyce who I miss more and more each day I thank you for your encouragement, support, editorial skills and critiques and for being the person behind the final stone.

Beneath these stones are many who deserve to be even deeper in the ground. Their lies and betrayals are so great that all the soil, tombs, coffins, and shovels used to create their graves could not prevent their lies from resurfacing. Each one has committed so many crimes of treachery, backstabbing, twisted acts of violence, deceptions, and betrayal that placing them beneath these onyx stones was just the first link to their permanent annihilation, obliterating them from the world. Some will just have simple markers to alert visitors to this cemetery that someone is buried in a particular grave. Others will be numbered, and some—those whose crimes were not directly caused by themselves but who were coerced or threatened into committing them by others—might have a simple plaque over their stone.

These stones are really quite valuable and more expensive than most. The faces behind these stones never really did anything wrong, but they probably deserve to be where they are. Hurting others, making fun of them even if you are just kidding, is inexcusable. Them not asking for forgiveness warrants what I did to each of the faces that lie, not so peacefully, behind each of these granite, marble, and in some cases onyx stones. My goal is to teach everyone a lesson...adults, teens, and young kids too. If you do not want to wind up as one of my precious faces behind one of these beautifully carved stones, then heed my warning.

Meet my driver...we will just call him Mr. Z. He drives my black limo with dark tinted windows, and he will guide you to the first stone. The stories will be told partially by me, and of course, partially by the victims. This first stone is in an older cemetery that is not kept very well. The caretaker sleeps most of the day in his shed and spends little time mowing the lawn or caring for the grounds. The grass looks overgrown and brown, and in some places you can see poison ivy; mildew covers the stones, and some look like the foundations need repair. The stones are mostly old, but his one has just been placed in the ground, and our star will tell you about him.

Those that are now behind these stones have much to atone for before they can be allowed to rest in peace. The lies they have told, the schemes they have created, cost many their lives, but few will be able to escape their punishment. One thinks that she will take on another star and be able to convince everyone she is more talented. Another man lies to his wife when he tells her that the infection she has is really nothing, and that she should just wait and see what happens. One reviewer will learn not to pan a book by a bestselling author because she's jealous that her own latest book never made the bestseller list. Bad reviews. You never know what lies are hidden beneath each of these stones.

But, there is much more that you will learn. So many lies are hidden beneath these stones. Only I can uncover them for you, and you will decide if the punishments fit the crimes.

FIRST STONE:
BURN: LET FLAMES REIGN!

Arson:
The crime of maliciously, voluntarily, and willfully
setting fire to the building, buildings, or other property
of another, or of burning one's own property for an
improper purpose, as to collect insurance.
Burn:
To undergo rapid combustion or consume fuel in
such a way as to give off heat, gases, and, usually, light;
be on fire.

I stood looking at that magnificent fire, watching
the flames soar and take over the entire building as the
structure was enveloped in a sea of orange, red, brown,
and then ash. Smelling the smoke, I saw the soot and
carnage that were created as my job was done—the
problem solved—and I left the scene, but not before I
watched the drama unfold. As the sirens blared in the
night air and the survivors of this fire alit from the
building, I saw fear, despair, and hopelessness on their

1

faces. This made me smile. Finally: the revenge I deserved for all they'd put me through.

My name was Jack and my hobby was arson, but not on buildings or businesses. I loved to create fires in homes, but not before making sure the people living there had insurance. You see, up until I was caught I had a good thing going. The people living in that rundown and dilapidated neighborhood were looking for ways to get out, make some money, and beat the insurance companies. Everyone knew that I was a fireman...it was true, but due to cutbacks some of the men in my house were laid off, given desk jobs for less money, or just encouraged to retire. In my case, I retired and took the package they offered.

But, I had expensive tastes and so did my wife Nelda. She loved her sports cars, furs, and designer shoes. She made a decent salary working in an office as a legal secretary to the president of a law firm, but she was selfish, greedy, and always wanted more. Nothing I ever did was good enough for her, and no matter how much I bought her she wanted more. So, I decided to help her get more; more space—lots of it, if you know what I mean.

My client was Mr. P, who was down on his luck and felt that he needed some help. But, I was not sure that I could trust him. Calling me on the cell phone that I had for just those special jobs, I arranged to meet him at the local pub at ten. After he left his office and met me there, we sat in the corner and hoped no one would overhear our conversation.

Mr. P laid out what he needed me to do and what he hoped the outcome would be. He had a garage where he kept wood for his fireplace and old leaves in a bag from the backyard. He had lighter fluid, matches, and other flammables on hand in case he wanted to burn his leaves, use his grill, or light his fireplace. But, Mr. P was going to get careless; or at least, he hoped *I* would become careless and make sure that his house burned to the ground...as long as no one would get hurt. We agreed on the date, time, and price for my services with a simple handshake. Now, I bet you think you have it figured out. Think again.

I went and bought all the supplies that I needed to complete the job and make sure that everything burned to the ground without anyone getting hurt or anyone being the wiser. The next morning I prepared my supplies and looked over my plans to execute the fire and make sure that everything was in place. I contacted the client and double checked the time, asked for a down payment, and went about preparing my supplies. Getting dressed quickly, I ate a quick snack and some coffee, then drove to the house in question.

I didn't see or hear anything from within the house, mostly because I was told to create the diversion and fire in the garage where all of the wood and flammables were kept. Using the lighter fluid, the matches, and the dried leaves that the owner had left in the garage instead of outside for pickup, I went about setting the fire. No one was around. His neighbors were out of town for a week, and the only other neighbor was an elderly lady who was in the hospital. Though it was a residential

3

area, very few houses were on each block, and trees and huge fences surrounded the area so it would be almost impossible to see another house, let alone inside their windows to where I was working. The best part of today was that it was cold and cloudy, and the sky was filled with dark cumulous clouds. Being a dead end street, only the cars that belonged to the man whose house I was in and one other would come down the street. No one was there as far I could see. The car that was in front of the vacant house I thought belonged to the woman in the hospital. Before I set the final match and lit the embers I rechecked everything, then I walked to my car and just waited.

The end came swiftly, and the house was soon enveloped in flames. The bushes around the perimeter were filled with dead leaves and the end result was a huge towering inferno. I made sure that the house was gone and that no evidence linked back to me, and I thought I was home free.

Getting back home and taking a shower to get all of the ash and smoke off me, I phoned the client and demanded payment. What happened next I never expected. Opening the door following the knock was my first and final mistake. Payment was made by Mr. P, but not in the way you think. After all, I was doing a service, getting the job done and the house burned, and the insurance money hopefully would be paid. But, some debts are often paid in full, and mine was paid as a Face Behind the Stones. My driver, Mr. Z, just smiled as he drove away with Mr. P in the back seat.

You see, had I looked up even for a minute when I was starting the fire, I might have seen a young girl at the window peering down at me. She never knew what happened as the flames spread, the windows blew out, and the end result you can only imagine. The basement was suppose to be empty too, but what can I say? Mr. P had not planned for his son's return from college, or his daughter returning a day early from a business trip. Their bodies were burned beyond recognition, but at least their ends came quickly.

***

Arson is wrong, and using it to collect insurance is more than wrong. In this case, many died as a result of my greed and the greed of one man. Others would follow, as someone else would take my place and earn the fee, but hopefully be more careful before they decided to let it burn. Arsonists are deadly and dangerous, and often do not get caught.

Fran Lewis

SECOND STONE:
THE FINGER: INFECTIONS CAN BE DEADLY

"Blood poisoning: The medical term is "septicemia." No matter which of these two terms—blood poisoning or septicemia—you prefer, what is meant is the same thing; namely, a "general (systemic) disease that is due to the presence and the persistence of germs (pathogenic microorganisms) or their toxins in the bloodstream." The "germs" can be bacteria (in bacteremia) or any other microscopic agent of infection capable of causing disease in humans. Another term that is very closely related to "blood poisoning" and "septicemia" is "sepsis." "Sepsis" also refers to the presence and persistence of germs or their toxins in the blood but those germs or toxins do not need to be in the blood. They may be in other tissues of the body. Blood poisoning/septicemia and sepsis are often serious. They can sometimes be life threatening diseases calling for urgent and comprehensive care."

7

Wound sepsis: sepsis originating from an infection of a wound.

Remember this as you read The Finger. My driver, Mr. Z, as I referred to him in the last story, is about to come to the next two stones, which belong to a married couple that you will meet. One is the grave of Harvey. Harvey thought that he would do away with his wife Sura in a unique and undetected fashion. But, Sura, who lies behind the second stone, will tell you the story and you decide for yourself: Murder, or just a case of too many germs and toxins in her blood?

One of the two stones is in the shape of a gold finger. The outline appears to be realistic, but the inner part of the finger is marred with a dark red line. The other stone is a plain concrete slab. Either Harvey or Sura just might wind up behind the fingered stone, and the other…well, just wait and see.

***

As Sura stepped out onto the pavement, her bulky weight making it difficult for her to move about, she started for the market but stopped. The pain in her right thumb was excruciating, and the redness and swelling on the lower part alarmed her and made her realize something was seriously wrong. But, when she had showed it to her husband Harvey before he left for work, he'd shrugged it off and told her to soak it in hot water and get busy with her day. Sura knew she had a serious problem, but she was too afraid to not complete her shopping, bring Harvey's cleaning to the cleaners, and walk the dog, because she never knew Harvey's moods and what would happen if she was late with anything he ordered her to do.

Walking to the cleaners, she began to feel faint and her body broke out in a cold sweat. But, she forged ahead.

***

My name is Sura and my story, unfortunately, landed me behind a magnificent stone; but let me tell you the rest...you just might be surprised.

Walking to the cleaners, I realized that something was seriously wrong with me but I knew that Harvey would check to see that his precious suits, ties, and jackets made it to Bright Star Cleaners. Mr. Wald was the owner and greeted me with his usual harsh tone and unfriendly smile. Leaving the cleaning on the counter, not needing a ticket, I started for the market but realized I could barely move.

I stopped and sat down on a bench that was in front of the bank, called my doctor, and asked for an appointment. Unfortunately, the receptionist did not think my problem was serious enough until I started to scream, rant, and rave about the pain, the fact that I knew I was burning up, and that my hand felt numb. I did not wait for her to answer; hanging up on her, I decided to drive myself to the office and dare them not to see me.

Walking into the doctor's office, I did not feel better but I felt that at least I might get to the bottom of the problem. I did not expect to see Harvey sitting there waiting for me. Why had she called him? What was going on, and why wouldn't he want me to be okay?

"Sura, I thought I told you not to go to the doctor, and that all you needed was to soak it in some hot water."

"I am my own boss, and don't tell me how to handle my health care. You just want me out of the way so you and Dedi can get it on more often without worrying about getting caught. You know, Harvey, I am on to you and your 400 pound whale of a girlfriend."

Harvey just looked at me in apparent disbelief as Dr. Jones came into the reception area and asked to speak to me alone. In the examination room, I explained the problem and showed him the line of red on my hand, and told him that I couldn't feel anything in some of my fingers. Looking closely, he told me that I did, indeed, have some type of blood poisoning, and that if I had not come to see him, I would probably have died.

***

Harvey paced up and down the waiting room. He called Dedi and told her their plan was foiled, hoping that no one heard him; but had they?

When Sura came out of the doctor's office, she smiled at Harvey and gave him a huge hug. "You know Harvey, I probably did overreact, but the doctor says that I do have blood poisoning. I am sure that you want it taken care of. Right?"

Acting all flustered and pretending to care about Sura, he hugged her tightly, too tightly, and whispered something in her ear which made her turn pale. But, she did not react until they were outside. "Harvey, try as you may you will not get away with what you are trying to do, and stop threatening me. If you want a divorce so

be it. But, I can assure you that you won't get
my inheritance or anything else."

"Don't be so sure."

What poor Sura did not know was that Harvey had
worked with her attorney and destroyed her will,
created a new one, and managed to get someone to
forge her signature, leaving all of her assets to him plus
giving him power of attorney. Sura would learn—but
too late—that she should have paid closer attention to
what Harvey was doing.

Going home together would prove to be a mistake
as Harvey realized that she was now under a doctor's
care, and he would have to think of something different
to rid the world of Sura so he could be with Dedi and
her four annoying and backstabbing kids.

***

But, Harvey did not realize that Sura was on to
him. Sura was concerned about her infection, and for
some reason the medicine that the doctor prescribed was
making her feel worse. Calling the pharmacy, she was
told the side effects of the medication, but for some
reason she had different ones. Looking at the bottle, she
even questioned the pharmacist and asked him to
describe the color of the capsules and what the dosage
should be in case the person that filled it had made a
mistake. What she learned was not surprising, but
would she be able to do anything about it in time?

When the pharmacist told Sarah the color of the
capsule and the name of the medication, she saw that
what he described was not what was on the bottle. Sura
had picked up the medication herself, but when she

arrived at the pharmacy the young man behind the counter had stated that he had to correct something before giving her the medication. Why? Sura described the man who gave her the meds to the head pharmacist, but he had no idea who it was since he was off that day and his partner, Hank, was there. Tom, the man behind the counter—if his name was really Tom—was either new, or something was seriously wrong.

Sura was feeling very tired, her muscles hurt, and she became short of breath. The pharmacist suggested that she call 911 or go to the ER, and at that moment the call was disconnected. Sura turned around and saw Harvey standing behind her with a sinister grin on his face, and Dedi right next to him.

***

I was feeling really sick, but the big fat blob that he was dating would not let me pass, and Harvey had that sick grin on his face, but something else was going on between them. I grabbed the bottle of medication and tried to get past both of them, but since she weighed as much as two beached whales and he had a knife in his hand, I was, as you might say, dead before my time. I saw it coming but I could not escape. The knife went right into my left side, but not before I took a hammer that was on the table and knocked him over the head.

Dedi tried to pour the rest of the pills down my throat. I would have thought she would be worried about Harvey. I began to float in and out of consciousness, but I knew I could not stay there and had to find a way out of my house and let someone know what Harvey had planned for me.

Dedi just stood there and grinned at Harvey and did not make a move to help him at all. When he looked up at her and begged her to call for help, she took the hammer and finished the job on him. But, there is always a twist of fate; sometimes you just never know who might wind up behind the stone, and who just might be telling the story.

Things happened in slow motion after that. I ran past Dedi while she was using the hammer to hack away at Harvey. I was in no position or shape to stop her. All the while she was laughing so loud I thought she would burst. Dedi was after only one thing, and that was Harvey's money, and of course mine. My will was safe in my lawyer's office, or so I thought. I never thought that Dexter Brown would betray a client and allow Harvey to change my will, leaving him all of my money. But, unfortunately for both of them, they would never collect.

Harvey never made it to the hospital…he died right there on the floor. Dedi thought she was going to get away scot-free, but I had put a video camera in my home to monitor it when I was not there. So, Ms. Dedi was the star of the movie titled, *I Killed Harvey For His Money*.

So, just how did I wind up behind this marble and granite stone? The medication was one reason, and the other might have been the fact that the knife was laced with some type of poison that got into my system. But, the end did not come so fast, and Dedi…well, she just might have gotten what she deserved. She loved to eat and did not care about her weight or her diet. Dedi was diabetic, and the only cakes in my house had tons of sugar, peanuts, and lots of chocolate. Dedi could not resist a good chocolate cake, but what she did not see were the walnuts in the center. I never ate the stuff…Harvey bought it all for himself.

Dedi could not resist taking a big slab of the cake, and…well, you probably know the rest. Her face turned a deep shade of red as she tried to find her EpiPen to inject the fluid in her leg to stop the allergic reaction to the nuts.

***

My name is Sura and what happened to me is really tragic…and the EpiPen is right here with me. Dedi is in another cemetery behind a huge stone that is unmarked. No one really cared about what happened to her…not Harvey, if he had survived, or even her kids. As far as my estate…well, since Harvey won't be around to collect because he, too, is behind a huge concrete stone somewhere, all of my money went to creating this monument to me. The stone that I am behind is made of solid marble, and the lettering is quite distinct and in gold.

Here lies Sura.
Go to hell Harvey:
Or are you there already?

STONE THREE:
ASHLEY HALL: SOAP STAR

The driver is in a unique and different cemetery. Those that are here are famous and have been on many television shows or movies. But, one stands out above the rest ...I think I will let Ashley tell you what happens herself, as you will learn in this particular stop that the driver is about to make. There are several faces that wind up behind the stone. Which one escapes the coffin you will have to figure out for yourself after reading *Ashley Hall: Soap Star*.

***

Ashley Hall was hot, smart, with a body that was perfectly fit and toned and a personality that no one wanted to mess with. On the outside, she appeared friendly, waved at her fans, and seemed so charming and nice. But, behind those icy blue eyes was a heart of stone. The effects of a tsunami were not as dangerous as the wrath of Ashley.

Ashley was the star of the soap *The Hot and the Sexy*. Her co-star, Brad Jones, was a male heartthrob,

15

and Ashley had at one time thought she played him like a violin. Around Ashley his strings would seem to unravel, and the end result would be that he was putty in her hands. On the set he deferred to her and the way she wanted scenes played. In the bedroom, he ruled only when she allowed him to…or so she thought.

Ashley loved to look at herself in the mirror and thought her appearance far surpassed anyone elses. Ashley hated competition and would destroy anyone that ever tried to steal her man. Brad, on the other hand, was hot to look at but had a real mean streak; a liar and a cheat, he actually played Ashley like an out of tune violin. The only thing was, she never knew it. So self absorbed and so full of herself, she never thought that any of the other female actor could hold a candle to her, or even come close.

But, Brenda Joy did. Brenda was tall and thin with long blonde hair. Her blue eyes sparkled and her figure was toned with not an ounce of fat, flab, or cellulite anywhere. Brenda appeared to be sweet, kind, and trusting on the outside, but she knew how to play the directors and producers.

Everyone on the set of her soap, including her director and leading man, hated Ashley Hall. But, Ashley knew things about all of them that kept them in line. Her director was having an affair with the producer. The leading man, as Ashley had discovered after ending her involvement with him, was having an affair with another leading man on another soap. Little did their wives know, nor would they know unless Ashley dropped hints or informed them in some way.

Well: Why not hear the story directly from her?

***

Brenda really got under my skin. She was a miss goody three shoes if you know what I mean, looking great all the time; but I was definitely better and hotter. As far as acting, she was as talented as a wet noodle. Babies that cried and acted out were more talented in getting their point across.

One day we were filming the murder scene. One of the main characters, Eloise, was getting knocked off the show, and none too soon for me. The actor's name was Marina Jones. She couldn't act, but she knew how to snort coke and light up those reefers. I got stuck sharing a dressing room with her out of the goodness of my heart, and all I heard every single day was for the old days of Woodstock, enjoyed living the hippie life, and wanted to go back to where it all began…wherever that was. She was a royal pain in the rear end, a whiner, and even more, at her age men still thought she was hot. Why? Who knew? There was no accounting for taste. So, how was I going to rid myself of this leech after she was finally knocked off the show? You see, they had decided to keep her on staff to help in the dressing rooms, the makeup rooms, and sets in order to keep her happy, because she knew stuff about some of the people working there that you can bet they didn't want to get out.

They called us to the set to discuss how the scenes would be filmed and in what order. But first, I had to figure out a way to rid myself of those two women forever. Murder was out of the question, but if by any chance they wound up dead, I wouldn't weep or cry…well, maybe just a few tears for effect. But, first I had to make an appearance to let everyone know that I was ready to do my scene with the leading man and assist in the murder on screen (don't worry; I promise I won't get caught).

Everyone was standing around waiting for the director to give us our cues and let us know when to begin. My role was to assist the leading man in kidnapping our victim and locking her in a room, chained to a bed to make sure she had no way to get out. Then, we were to enter and administer a drug that would take care of the rest and hopefully not be found in her blood stream. But, fret not, if they were able to tell how she died we would make it look like a drug overdose. Everyone knew that Eloise was a drug addict and couldn't stay clean for more than a minute.

As the scene began we managed to lure the victim to our car under the pretense of wanting to talk to her about a case that we were investigating. That was what made this so sweet and simple. I was Detective Smith and my partner was Detective Jones. Luring Eloise into the police car was easy. Convincing her we would try and get her something to make her feel better even easier. But, why would two cops want to take out an over the hill drug addict?

That's for you to learn when you watch the soap.

But, back to more important things. The scene was filmed and we were about to film the next part when I noticed something on the ceiling of the room that we were filming in…a camera that caught everything we did. So, the director was going to allow us to commit murder and think we were getting away with it when in reality he was trying to rid the show of us too. Not going to happen. Good thing I was paying close attention to what was around me and I had a keen eye for details. So, what was I going to do in order to turn things in my favor? After all, I was great at what I did. Marina was smart, and although the director thought this was just a scene in the show, what was going to happen was murder.

Just who would be sacrificed next, and didn't the director know I wouldn't hesitate to use what I had on him and invent some more to get what I wanted? I decided to make sure that he paid for his actions, and that Brenda learned not to mess with me too.

The scenes were filmed and the next day's script handed out, and what I saw really made me fume. What he had in mind for me—and not for Brenda— was inexcusable, and I could not understand why until I overheard the two of them laughing and talking about me. Brenda was having her own fun with the director, and they both thought I would not find out they wanted me off the show so she could take the leading role. Not in this lifetime.

As the door to the director's trailer opened, I sauntered past them and just waved. No one realized that I had overheard him or her, and no one knew what I would do next. Calling my friend Jack on his cell phone, I put my plan into motion. Jack met me outside of the studio and handed me what I needed to make sure that Brenda and the director got what they deserved.

(Just what he handed me you won't find out just yet, or not until the final curtain falls on all of them during the first scene tomorrow.)

Brenda was going to try out in the soap for a part in a cosmetic commercial as part of her career on the soap. She played an actress who could not seem to get a part in a movie, and she did commercials and short films to get by. This commercial was for a face cream that was supposed to eliminate wrinkles and fine lines. The cream was called Smooth Face, and the end result should yield a smoother face minus the wrinkles and fine lines after about eight weeks of using the cream. Just how would this benefit me? (Wait and see what I do, and what is in the cream that I will make sure she uses during the show.)

The next morning we were all on the set and the final scenes were rehearsed as the director explained Brenda's role, her scene, and the fact that one or more of us would be cut and the final scenes for those either just leaving the show or killed off would not happen for another month. Brenda entered the studio, and was given the cream that she was supposed to use during the commercial with the director of the show or the actor that had that part. Something went wrong with the lighting, and all of a sudden everything went dark and no one moved, afraid they would knock something over that would bump into the cameras. Putting on the night vision goggles that I had "borrowed" from my brother the cop, I carefully switched the creams.

When the lights came back up no one was the wiser since both jars looked exactly the same, but the end result...well, that's something you'd have to see for yourself. The scene began and I, Ashley, stood off to the side since I was not in the scene. As the scene opened, Brenda began her demonstration and applied the cream to her face, but nothing happened at first. I just stood by and watched as all of a sudden she began to itch, then scream that her face was on fire. The rest you would have to be there to believe as the skin on her face peeled off, leaving her cheeks blood red, and the ambulance was called; but the end result was not pretty.

So, how did I wind up behind the stone and why am I not the star of the soap anymore?

Sometimes family members are really not exactly on your side, and when my brother found his goggles missing and thought I took them, he decided to learn more about what happened to Brenda. When my brother realized that they were missing, what would have given him the impression that I had anything to do with Brenda's accident?

The people on the show blamed it on the company that made the cream. Brenda never really got back to herself even after many skin grafts and surgeries. Her career was over; but who really cared about her? I was just trying to keep my job and not be outclassed or kicked aside. Ashley Hall was no one to fool with, and you definitely did not want to cross me.

But, someone decided that they wanted me out of the way to make room for another star, and that killing me off the show was not going to do it. Someone really hated me, and the blackmail notes arrived saying that they knew what I did to Brenda. But, I never flinched and I never gave anything away.

***

Reporting for work as usual, I surveyed the behavior of the other actors and tried to figure out who'd sent the typed message. I never found out. My days on the soap were numbered, as I read the scenes for that week and realized my character was about to be killed off in a boating accident. But, I would not go down lightly.

The end result you can figure out...the accident looked real, and the scene was staged. Even though the coroner said it was a malfunction in the engine and that the steering wheel on the motor boat was not working correctly, the fact that I was alone on the boat with no life jacket and no way to communicate should tell you something.

I am Ashley Hall: Now I am the most beautiful face behind the stones. Lies beneath the stones will never be uncovered, and no one will ever know what I did.

Except you! And you won't tell: Will You? Would you like a jar of face cream?

STONE FOUR:
THE REVIEWER: ONE BAD REVIEW TOO MANY

As the driver heads to Beth Tom Cemetery, you will learn who is behind the star shaped stones made out of onyx and the cross-shaped ones made of bronze.

***

Katarina Valente was a book reviewer with a scrupulous reputation for destroying authors and novels that she felt were unworthy of being in print. Katarina was ruthless and mean, and got paid thousands of dollars by magazines and newspapers to not only review the books, but also create commentaries on the authors' life styles and writings.

Before becoming a book reviewer she'd had a shady past. She was a groupie, played lead guitar in a band, and enjoyed going to Woodstock and living in a commune. Katarina was a wild young woman, but as an older adult she had become hardened to life, and developed no sense of right or wrong. (When you learn more as she tells you her story, you decide if she got what she deserved.)

Katarina reviewed all genres, but when her nemesis Matilda G—the number one book reviewer in the world—decided to pen her first novel, Katarina decided this might be her chance to take over the top spot and destroy Matilda's reputation as a writer. So, rather than ask her for the honor of reviewing it, she carefully downloaded the book on her Kindle.

Fight to the Finish was the title of Matilda's book, a story based on real life events of her son who had been a boxer and died in the ring. But, Katarina did not care about the plot, the story, or the title. She was out to make sure that this novel never reached the Times bestseller list or any list at all.

Matilda also seemed to be trying to destroy Katarina's reputation as a reviewer. Matilda would read some of her reviews, and if Katarina did not ask to receive emails when readers commented on her reviews, she would not know what this cruel and vindictive person was saying about them. She implied that Katarina did not read the books and just reworded other reviews, back covers, or blurbs on the inside flaps. Katarina also read Matilda's reviews, but was more subtle and clever in her commenting. Matilda was fearless, but Katarina was flawless up until this point.

Book reviewers take a big chance when an author sends them their titles to review. If they give the author their home address, they chance being found if they give the author a really negative review. They risk being harassed, threatened, and even hurt if found, and this reviewer was no different. Clever, smart, and not really honest, Katarina would review over ten titles in about three hours, claiming she was a speed-reader. Truth be told she never read anything; she paid her assistant to help her by outlining the plot and the characters and providing a short summary of the book, which was just enough for her to create the review for the author.

Matilda was after Katarina for many reasons, least of all her book and her title. Katarina was tall, thin, and really gorgeous, while Matilda would need weeks on Slim-Fast, Weight Watchers, and Jenny Craig before even making a dent in her 340 pound frame. Matilda spent much of her time munching on candy and eating chips, while Katarina read, walked, and perfected her reviews, even if she was only reading the back cover and rewording it. Matilda was right about her methods. She never finished a book unless it was under three hundred pages, but she was considered a great reviewer and speed reader...one of the best.

Katarina had just completed a review of a new murder mystery and was posting it on several sites for other reviewers, readers, and authors to read before posting it on Amazon and Shelfari. Katarina felt that the book was worthy of anything but five stars; if the author was lucky, she might eke out two. The plot line was weak, the characters were flawed, the ending was not possible, and the storyline put the reviewer to sleep at times. Added to that, the book was over four hundred pages too long, and the main character was quite irritating, annoying, and definitely not anyone you could or would identify with. She said this and more in her review.

But, what Katarina did not know was the real name of the author of the book titled *Murder At Midnight* by Jasmine White Green. Little did she know that her nemesis had written the book under this pen name just to find out what people really thought about her work without revealing who she really was.

While Katarina was reading, posting, editing, and writing her review of *Murder At Midnight,* the author was plotting something awful against her. Hacking into Katarina's computer files, Matilda was able to not only read the review that she'd written, but alter it without Katarina's knowledge. Katarina would do an overview of her reviews but Matilda was the real brains behind the final copy. Never realizing that was Matilda was changing her words, her thoughts, and her rating, Katarina was also blindsided by her assistant.

Although her assistant was supposed to edit, revise, and make sure Katarina's reviews were perfect, she hated Katarina to the point that she began sabotaging her reviews. The woman would make sure that something was missing in each review, that at least one typo was left in, and hoped someone would notice the errors in the plot synopsis that would signal that Katarina never read the book. The woman was smart, crafty and she thought slick. As her assistant she did her best to undermine Katarina and make sure that the reviews were poorly edited, making her look bad.

But our reviewer was smart, and before posting her words and thoughts she always did one more read through for typos, spoilers, and grammar errors. When reading the reviews she realized that certain phrases were out of context, that some of what was written she would never write, and several of the negative comments were missing. She had given Murder At Midnight three stars, and for some reason this review said five golden ones. Not understanding what really happened and thinking that she might have accidentally changed some of her own thoughts she rewrote the review, changed it back to what she wanted to say, and saved it on a flash drive.

But, Matilda had her own thoughts and would not give up. Posting some negative things about Katarina on Facebook and My Space was just the beginning. Stating that Katarina never read the books she reviewed, could not write a review for dust, and had poor writing skills was just the start of her war to take down this reviewer. So, who would win? Which one found her way behind the next stone?

Katarina worked the late shift in a bookstore, which allowed her to use her days to write her reviews, write and proofread her books, and get her chores done. She was also writing her next murder/mystery which was about to be released. Working late was okay with her.

But getting blindsided when she left the bookstore…well, this was how it went down. Walking outside, she hailed a cab because she did not drive alone at night. Getting into the cab, she did not notice the driver's face before telling the person behind the wheel where she was going and giving her address. More concerned about telling her husband she was on the way home, she texted him with her intended arrival time, not realizing that this just might be the only clue as to her whereabouts when she was reported missing.

***

When she did not arrive home at the set time, her husband went outside to wait for the cab. Texting Katarina, he received an odd response: *You won't find her. She is now mine. Her life is over and you need to move on.*

Terrified, John, her husband, called the police and informed them of what the text said and hoped that the GPS on her phone would help locate where she might be. No one thought to question Matilda, because no one really knew about their feud.

Matilda's novel had gotten some good press, but then she was the one writing her own reviews, and paying people to write positive ones so she would hopefully find her way on to the bestseller list.

***

But, what happens you won't believe…the harsh reality when another finds you out and wants to take you down.

Katarina is vengeful and would do anything to strike back at a competitor or someone she considers an enemy. So, where is she and who texted John? Was it Matilda? Was it someone else that decided to rid the world of this talented but jealous reviewer that did not like to be considered anything less than number one? Where was Katarina?

Listen carefully and you will hear the sounds of typing, nails clicking away on the keyboard, and the

28

loud screams coming from a voice that can no longer be heard. Hidden away in a dark and deserted place, hoping to be found, chained to a chair you will find our reviewer, who now just writes, types, and reviews for one author. Can you guess which one? Just who is behind the stone? Whose voice and spirit will you hear when you pass the gold stone that says, "The Reviewer"? You decide, because this note came right after John received the text: *Some authors need to be silenced and their writing permanently deleted.*

Who wrote this note? You decide, but don't look for either one of these authors to write anything new anytime soon.

Signed: The Deleter

STONE FOUR:
HAROLD: CRIME PAYS IF YOU DON'T GET CAUGHT

Did you ever watch the show *Dead Like Me*? The characters are great and the premise of the show is really quite unique. Someone dies, whether they deserve to or not, and the character takes their soul. In the show the characters come back with different faces, but after taking a soul of the person they have been assigned to they wait with them until they cross over to the other side.

Well, I was on my way to work and stopped into a coffee shop for my morning caffeine fix. A young man was standing right outside the door. Opening the door for me, I just thought he was being polite. Little did I know he was sent by someone else to make sure that I never got to work or anywhere else ever again.

My problem is that now I am in Limbo, somewhere in a room with stale air, thick walls and…well you can read the rest. They said my crimes were so heinous that

I did not deserve to go to Heaven, and Hell might not be hot enough for me. So, right now I am in a new place that they created for those of us that do not deserve to be anywhere. It's not quite Purgatory but close enough. My name is Harold. This is my story. You, the reader can decide where I belong.

I am telling this story from behind the four walls of the mausoleum that I have been locked away in. The walls are thick, and of course there is no air supply. How did I wind up here and not behind one of those fancy stones? This is a small room. I even get to share it with another coffin. This is where it all ended, as you'll see when I tell you my story and explain what I did.

***

I was sitting on a couch in a plain room, with nothing but four blank walls and a door facing me and staring me in the face. Things were different in the world now. Buildings had no windows, fresh air was pumped in through vents, cars were battery operated, and the outside world did not exist for me.

My name was Harold, and I was the founder of an Internet company www.justaskharoldandhe'lltellyou.com. Harold—that is, I—was the sole founder and owner of this company. People from everywhere in the world would email me, text me, and call for advice regarding just about every get rich quick scheme. I controlled the markets and told stockbrokers which stocks were hot, which were cold. I gave advice to rich executives who needed to make investments in order to liquidate funds and get some quick cash. My clients made millions, and so did I. For a monthly fee and a large commission, these rich executives were able to make these investments and no one knew where or how they were made. Hidden bank accounts were untraceable and everyone was happy, especially me.

I was fifty years old and a genius. I understood the market, playing the horses, slots, and any game of chance. I could tell you how to beat the odds at a roulette table. I could even teach you how to count cards in Black Jack. Therefore, why was I sitting there in a room with four walls, locked away, never to see the outside world again? Because, somehow, someway, I was caught. I had only one chance for escape

Sitting there contemplating my fate, I began to see flashes of things to come...or were they? Looking at a wall, I saw a man who looked just like me, but it was not me. He had a wife and family and looked fairly well off. Then, the vision disappeared.

I began thinking of what I should do next. There were no windows where I was. There was one door but it was bolted shut, and the only contact I had with anyone was through a small vent in the ceiling. All of my belongings were taken from me when I was placed in this room. It was neither my final stop nor where I would remain for the rest of my sorry, miserable life. It was called the Limbo Room, where someone stayed either until they figured out what would happen next, or until their captors did it for them.

Sitting at the small desk in the room, I began to see some more of the vision from before. I saw the man at work, and I wanted to learn more about his life and what he did.

He was sitting behind a large desk in an office with plush carpeting and huge bay windows, with a cappuccino machine and his own twenty-five-year-old secretary. Wearing a black suit, steel grey shirt, and tie, he looked polished and ready for whatever he was supposed to be doing. Then, the vision disappeared and I saw the blank wall in front of me.

I had been a mogul of industry. Presidents of countries would use my website to help them make major oil deals, decide whether to purchase companies, and discover where to get weapons for their armies to fight other countries. I was paid handsomely and never discussed my clients with anyone. I worked alone, except for a small staff of people that watched the markets in every country for me, checked oil prices around the world, and dealt with those in charge of selling weapons that were needed by my major clients. Not all of these people left their offices to go home. Everyone lived in the building where my company was. They were all carefully investigated, and were required to sign some special forms before being hired swearing never to divulge what they did for my company. Any outside friends or family were not told what they did, nor did they have any contact with these people as long as they worked for me. Therefore, how was I caught and what was my downfall? Why did I think my life was so great? It was not now, and they would be coming for me soon. I was not going to remain in Limbo much longer.

However, before I left I had to figure out who this man was and what he had to do with my future.

Time moved slowly. I was sitting facing the back wall, and this time the vision was clearer. I could hear voices and what people were saying. This man's name was also Harold, and he was a bank president with a wife, two children, and a girlfriend. He was not only the president of the bank, but he controlled what investments the money in the bank was used for and where the profits went. I heard him on the phone with the CFO and the CEO of the bank, discussing a possible takeover of another bank.

The vision disappeared again, but now I had some idea where I might fit in and how I might not be in Limbo forever. However, first I needed to learn more about this man...who he was, where he lived, and how his life would make mine better. Staring at the wall, I hoped to see something, but I did not.

A voice from the vent called, "Harold, you have twenty-four hours to go, and then your fate will be decided. Do you understand?" I did not bother to answer. It did not require a response. They could read my mind and if they did, they would not like what they heard. However, give up I would not, and focus and concentrate I would.

I had never been satisfied with my life. I was never happy until I created the Internet company, and even then, I was still dissatisfied with my life. Not very handsome and never really noticed when walking down the street, I decided to make myself more marketable and more noticeable by starting this company and helping people get rich. Starting the company and creating the website was easy. Advertising on YouTube, Face Book, and other sites helped to get the word out that I was there to help anyone that had money to invest and needed to do it quickly and quietly without the knowledge of the IRS or anyone else in government.

I was getting tired but I could not sleep…my survival depended on figuring out who this man was and why he was important to me.

The vision was clearer now. I saw him at home with his wife and family. He had dinner, went into his study, and made several calls. "I need you to take five million dollars and invest it for me in Company A. I then need you to take five million more and invest it in Company B. When you are done and the money is where I want it and the investments are made, I want you to sell both of them off. No, you do not use company money, you use the money in the client funds and make sure you tell no one. My wife wants a new car, my girls want to go on several trips, and I want to make it happen. Do whatever you have to do and get those investments made, and make sure when the stocks go up you sell them electronically and transfer the money into my special account. The clients…well, they will be none the wiser. Do not record any of this in his or her portfolios, and do not discuss this with anyone. Remember, you owe me and I can destroy you with one phone call."

The man in the room and what he was doing were no different from what I had done…but he had not been caught. He was using client money to fund his own investments. His wife had inherited a lot of money from an aunt that died, and he had embezzled all of it for his own purposes. She had no idea. As long as he kept her happy and gave her whatever she wanted, she would never question what he was doing with her money or where it was going.

As he sat there waiting for the phone call, his cell phone rang. It was his secretary, otherwise known as the girlfriend he wanted to dump. She was becoming too demanding and wanted a permanent position in his life, but he had it too good at this time and was not going to make any changes just yet.

The vision disappeared, and a voice came from the vent saying, "You have five more hours, and then it is over." I felt my body shake and hoped that the vision would appear one more time so that I would know the final outcome and what I had to in order to get out of limbo.

Staring straight at the wall, I began to feel a little strange. My arms started to tingle and I felt faint. Since there was just a small cot for me to rest on, I had no choice but to lie down on the hard metal floor. I started to shiver and shake all over, uncontrollably. What had they put in my daily meal? What had they put through in the air in the vent? Was this the end, or was it something else? Maybe I was not going to escape my fate. Maybe this was where I would spend eternity for what I had done.

After a few minutes, the shaking stopped and I felt better. I heard the voice say, "Four more hours and then…." Looking straight at the wall, I could hear the man speaking, and hoped that now all would finally be revealed.

The voice coming out of the vent in my cell said, "Listen carefully, Harold… you will hear this only once and see it in a flash. Remember all details or you will lose and go somewhere much worse than Limbo. Heed my warning."

I looked at the man in the vision and studied his mannerisms and what he was doing. I heard him say the same things to people that I had said before being caught. "Do not worry, that new shipment of cars with the hybrid engines was already sent with the extra packages in the trunks." "Do not worry, the stocks you wanted purchased were acquired, and will be worth twice as much in the morning." "Do not worry, Mr. President, no one will know." "Do not worry, Mr. Ambassador, I will never tell."

Then all of a sudden I realized something.

All of my life I was smart. All of my life I did the right thing and towed the mark. I helped all of these people get rich. I helped them using every trick I knew and every get rich quick method I knew. So, why was I there? I was just a plain and ordinary man. I never complained about my life, dull as it was. Even though I made others rich—and myself too—it became routine and boring after a while. I must have given someone the wrong tip, or the wrong person a good stock tip…or more.

The final vision began to appear…it was now or never to find out what I had to do. Staring straight at the man, I heard and saw him quite clearly. Sitting behind his huge oak desk and dictating a letter to someone, his cell phone rang. Listening to the person on the phone, we both heard the same thing. The man's face turned white. He dropped the phone on the floor and just stared at the door in front of him. The person on the phone had said he would pay for what he did. He said the tip he'd given him had cost him everything and more. This was his end.

Time seemed to race ahead and the next thing I knew the voice coming from the vent said, "You have been here ten years, and it is now 2030 and your time in Limbo is up. Did you figure it out yet? You have had all this time to learn what you need to do to get out.

"Look ahead and see your fate or remain...."

The man in the vision was in a room just like mine, chained to the chair. Three people were in the room interrogating him.

"I swear I never smuggled drugs or sold rare gems to foreign leaders. I never embezzled money from my clients or stole from their portfolios. I never took or gave bad stock tips. I invested in the same things they did and in the same companies. I even gave them shares in my company. I watched how he did it all those years. I kept a close eye on everything he did. I am even using his website...www.justaskharoldandhe'lltellyou.com. I did not change anything. I even had my surgeon make me look like him. I hated him all my life and I still hate him. I was the one who everyone thought would amount to nothing. I was the one who followed the rules and never got in trouble. How could this happen? I am just a fifty-year-old investment counselor who got caught up in the frenzy."

Listening to them speak, I realized what I had to do and I hoped it would work. Staring straight at the wall and watching what looked like a live video feed from an interrogation room, I saw the three men turn the man to face the wall and tell him to walk toward it and not stop when he came face to face with it. As he walked toward the wall, I walked in the direction of the wall that was facing me.

***

Harold from the vision began to feel dizzy and his face broke out in a sweat. The vent that was blowing fresh air into the room was no longer blowing fresh air. Someone was filtering in a lethal poisonous gas and Harold…well, now you know why his four walls became another four, but this time with no escape.

***

The next thing I knew I was sitting in his house and in his chair, with his wife and family. He was where I used to me, in Limbo or worse. I was now him and he was now me. This time I would do things to help those that needed stock tips, investments, and more. BUT THIS TIME I WOULD NOT GET CAUGHT! I would even set up a new website and make sure no one traced it back to me or knew it was me.

***

www.ididithaha.com is now in business and you can ask me anything.

The time has come and the end is here. Just where I will wind up has yet to be determined. After reading my story and hearing my voice, where do you think I should go?

Harold!

A Journey to Nowhere: Who Gets the Final Stone?

Sometimes life takes us in many different directions, as one man finds out. The final stone will take you to another time period and place, and teach many never to take life for granted, to pay closer attention to what is right in front of them, and never ever trust strangers.

***

All I had with me was my suitcase and the clothes on my back. I looked straight ahead of me and saw an endless dirt road, which extended for miles and miles. Wearing my lucky old beat up hat and my woolen coat, I left home early that morning to decide my fate.

My day began with breakfast, going to work at the bank, and coming home to an all but empty apartment with just my faithful dog for company. I felt as though I was going through the motions of life, and my life resembled watching an old movie or rerun of a television program every day. Life became mundane with no challenges ahead and nothing to look forward to. I got up at the same time every day, went to work, and came home. I was a bank president...I ran the largest bank in town. It was not a very exciting job, but the money was good and it paid for my kids' school tuition fees and their various extra-curricular activities. There was even money for my soon to be ex-wife to shop wherever and whenever she wanted.

My wife, who never had to work a day in her life, said she was bored and I provided her with no excitement. She had been going to the gym, working out, and met someone else there. She decided to take herself and my children and go to live with this total stranger after knowing him for just one month. She even managed to get herself a job as a copy editor at the local newspaper in the area where she was moving to. The man she met was the paper's editor, and I could not see how his job was any more exciting than mine was. However, he was ten years younger than me, and that seemed to be the draw.

Watching them leave, and feeling a tangled mixture of emotions, I realized that I could not make a difference in other people's lives, so I needed to start with my own. Staring into her new paramour's face as he got into his car with my family, I had an uneasy feeling. His eyes stared straight at me and his smile was cold and frightening, but he did not speak directly to me. He looked evil, and my kids were shaking with fear. My wife told me it would be better this way, got into the car, and never looked back.

I stood there staring at the back of the car until it disappeared. I could not believe what had happened, nor would I ever believe that I had no choice but to let it. My children were my life and I could not think about living the rest of it without them. However, Jana felt that since I bored her to death with talk of my days at the bank, and nothing much ever happened to excite her during hers, this young guy, whose face looked cold and demonic, was the right one for her. It was as if he had her under a spell.

I began to think of places where I could go and where I would spend the rest of my life, but I couldn't think that far ahead. I wandered down the road until I came to a small body of water that was surrounded by trees and grass. There was no one in sight. It was pitch black, and the sky was covered with clouds so dark and ominous that I stood frozen to the spot and couldn't move. The air was damp, and yet I felt nothing. I was neither hot nor cold…I felt numb. Feeling nothing but pain in my heart and fear that someone would finally find me and make me go back to the life I had before, I knew that I had to make a move in some direction.

I began contemplating my next step. I didn't know where I was or where the road would lead me, and it was so dark that I decided to stay where I was until morning.

However, that decision was not so easy to fulfill. I saw headlights coming towards me from a distance. I hid behind a tree, or at least I tried to, but I was wearing a yellow shirt and the driver must have seen me from a distance. He got out and walked in my direction. Being in an isolated area, I didn't know where to go or where to run, so I just stood there like a statue hoping that I would look like part of the scenery. As he came closer, I realized that he was a police officer and might recognize me and take me back home.

He drew closer, but before he could approach close enough to speak I heard the crackling of his radio, and he stopped in his tracks, but not before looking me straight in the eye with his cold eyes and icy stare. His smile sent chills down my spine, and I prayed he would not come any closer.

He turned back in my direction before leaving. I thought for a minute that he was the same man who had taken my family away from me. However, from a distance I could not be sure.

I passed the night in that place, rooted to the spot, afraid and unsure of myself. With the coming of daylight I summoned what remained of my courage and made my way home. That very day, things began to change.

My head began to hurt and I couldn't see where I was going. I had just been to the eye doctor, who had given me a new prescription for distance glasses. He assured me that wearing them would make things look much clearer. The glasses would help me not only see where I was, but also, possibly, "where I needed to go." That remark seemed strange at the time, but I just thought he was trying to make me feel better. Little did I know that things would change radically for me and I would have no idea how or why.

Putting on the new glasses and perusing my surroundings, I decided yet again to get away from home and its memories. I began walking, with no idea where I might end up.

After what seemed like about an hour, I came to what I thought was a small town. Everything in the town was new and in pristine condition. All of the people were older and looked like they were going about their business without noticing or stopping to speak with anyone who came their way. Everyone was dressed alike, everyone looked alike, and yet no one said a word. All of the stores were well kept, and had one person standing at a cash register waiting to check out an order, but no one entered any of the stores.

I began adjusting my glasses to make sure that I was seeing clearly when someone tapped me on the shoulder.

"Why aren't you in your proper place, and why are you just wandering around doing nothing? Don't you know that is not the way we do things here? Haven't you been here long enough?"

The man didn't introduce himself nor did he stop to hear my response. He just kept on going, saying the same thing.

"There is no hope for our young people today. So irresponsible, so undependable, and so worthless."

I walked a little further, stopped, and stared at myself in a store window. Staring back at me was a younger man dressed like all of the other people in the town, but it was still me, looking at least ten years younger. It seemed that the man knew who I was, or at least he was pretending to know me, but he never called me by name, told me where I was, or said what he thought I was supposed to be doing.

The entire town was about ten blocks long and about five blocks wide. Each block had three or four stores and three or four small houses. Behind each of the stores were wooded areas, and behind that what looked like gated communities. No one seemed to notice or care that I was there...except for that one person.

As I came to the end of the town, I could not believe what I saw. A sign read "You are leaving the town of Mundane and No Excitement: Today's Date is January 25, 2025."

What had happened to me in between? When I left home, it was 2010. Where had fifteen years gone, and where was I during those years?

Walking out of the town, I came to a fork in the road, where I saw four signs.

The first one read, "The road to the town of nowhere: Keep wandering."

The second read, "The road to the town of decisions."

The third announced itself as, "The road to the town of surprises."

And the fourth, "Just walk in this direction and you will find out."

I had no idea what these signs really meant, and since I was really nowhere that I knew, I thought about taking off my glasses and hoping to find myself back where I'd started and in my own home town. When I did, nothing changed, so I started walking in the direction of the second town, hoping that this town of decisions would help me make some for myself. However, when I got there, I knew things were only going to get worse.

At the entrance of the town was the man who had taken my family. Facing me with his cold stare and chalky face, he stood there all alone and smiled.

"Where are my kids and Jana?" I asked.

He just stared at me as if I was invisible and then vanished into thin air. I looked around and saw nothing, until I looked straight ahead of me to where he'd been standing and saw something so frightening that I thought I might be hallucinating. I beheld a vision...I could see what looked like a floating ball, and inside the ball I could see my family.

However, they were no longer my family; they were now his. Each one had been transformed into a carbon copy of this demonic creature. Each sat on a chair or bed staring into space with a strange grin on his/her face...just blank stares, like they were drugged or under some kind of spell. Then the vision disappeared. Frightened to think or even move, I just stood where I was and I took off my glasses. I began looking around, and I was no longer in the town but on the same road I was walking on when I left home.

I sat down in the middle of road and started to cry. Where was I, and what was happening?

All of a sudden, I heard voices, loud yells, and screams.

"Happy New Year. It is now the year 2200, and what a great world it is. Welcome to the next century."

49

Where had the time gone? I'd just been in the year 2025. It seemed that every time I left a place I was sent even further into the future.

I might have been on the same road that I started my journey on, but my surroundings were different. Instead of the beautiful houses and trees in the once countrified community that I had lived in, the area was totally devoid of any trees, vegetation, or houses. The road was no longer paved, but instead was constructed from hard stones and pebbles. The surrounding area featured burnt out barns and houses that were in total disrepair. I walked along this road hoping to find a small town or any sign of people. What I did find was so frightening I froze.

In front of me was a community of small children who looked like they were all alone with no adults in sight. They seemed to be part of some colony. The oldest of these children looked to be about sixteen years old. The rest of the children were lined up in front of me, and one other person that looked about sixteen years of age seemed to be in charge.

"Everyone here has a job to do. You will follow our orders. If you disobey, you will be severely punished. None of your parents survived the fire or the attack on this village. You have no other place to go. Everyone here must band together and try to make this place our home. You will have chores to do and some studies that we decide you must learn. You will also cook and clean for yourselves. Hunting and gathering food is your job if you want to eat and stay alive. There are no more supermarkets, restaurants, or even convenience stores.

We do have a small general store where our small community can get certain things that we need. However, there are many animals that you can kill and hunt down and eat. We are lucky to have several cows that can be milked, and some hens that might lay some eggs. You are here and that is all there is to it. Everyone must get to work to build a shelter to live in or use whatever houses are here. You can rebuild something or just start from scratch. I do not care. Just remember, we are a community and we must stick together and protect ourselves from any strangers from any other villages or cities that might try and come here and take what little we have."

Just as he was about to turn back and go into his house, or what appeared as a small house, he saw me standing there looking straight into his cold eyes. I could not believe it. The face that was staring straight at me was a younger version of the man who had taken my family away so many years ago. This person must be his descendant. I froze where I was standing. However, he said nothing. Maybe they couldn't see me clearly, but I could see them.

How could the future of the world turn into what looked like the past? As I was propelled into the future, it felt like the world was moving backwards in time.

As I stood watching the scene before me, someone must have come up from behind, hit me on the head with something hard, and knocked me out. When I finally woke up, I had a throbbing headache, felt nauseous, and could barely sit up. The left side of my face and head were covered in dried blood. Whatever I was knocked out with had had a sharp edge and really did some major damage to my head and my face. I could not stand up without feeling dizzy and light-headed.

I did not see anyone around. My eyes were having trouble focusing on where I was and my vision was blurry. What had happened to the village and the community where I saw the strange boy?

When my vision finally cleared and the throbbing in my head seemed to be subsiding, I took a long look at my surroundings. I was no longer in the same place I was before I was knocked out. I was in an open field with nothing but grass and farmland in the distance. I could not see any barns, farmhouses, or anything. There was no one in sight as far as I could see.

When I was finally able to stand I knew I needed to decide which way to go. Where should I walk and in what direction? However, all I saw on all four sides were empty fields of green for miles around.

Then out of nowhere, I saw an object coming at me at a high speed from a distance. I tried to get out of its way but I had no idea what it was or who was controlling it.

In a flash and a blur, someone grabbed my arms and my legs, I was thrown into a vehicle, and something was placed over my head. I could not see anything at all. I tried to scream but nothing came out of my mouth.

After what seemed an age the vehicle stopped, and when I was finally taken out of the vehicle and my eyes uncovered, I was no longer in the village with the children, nor was I in the town of Boredom and

Mundane. This was somewhere else. There were people standing on moving sidewalks and cars of sorts that were going at warp speeds high in the air and flying over other layers of traffic. People on phones were able to not only talk to the person but see them as well. The stores' and the shops' clerks and managers did not look human. They looked like droids of some kind. The people had odd stares and their faces seemed fixed with one expression. No one noticed me or seemed to realize that I was different.

Hanging in mid air was a calendar that said, "Today is January 25, the year is 3000. It will be warm and sunny today just like yesterday and tomorrow. The temperature will be 75 degrees today just like yesterday and tomorrow. The name of this town is Stand Still."

I began to rethink what had happened to me so far and realized that in every place I had been the date was the same but the year had changed each time.

Just as I was about to try and leave the town, I saw the demonic face and cold stare of a young man who seemed frozen in time standing right in front of me. He had not aged at all. His appearance was the same as it was when he had come and taken my family away from me. Behind him were my Jana and my children, all looking straight at me with that same cold stare and drugged smile.

As I stood, uncomprehending and afraid, a voice from somewhere in my dim memory spoke softly from the deepest recesses of my mind.

Welcome to Your Life: the places might change, the date will stay the same, and the GLASSES will determine what happens to you: You see: I am the Eye Doctor! Do you see things clearly now?

***

When he takes off the glasses and realizes where he really winds up, you will know just who finds their way behind the last stone. Families are gone. Lives have changed, and the years have moved ahead. But, when choices are made that are wrong and you find yourself having to rethink your life, one wrong decision, one lie, one betrayal, and you, too, will wind up behind the next stone.

THE FINAL BETRAYAL:
MJ WALSH RETURNS

I know that I have been gone for quite some time, but my spirit lingers on. I cannot rest until I find out, and you find out, what really happened to me, and why Marvin found it necessary to finally pull the plug on his beloved wife—that's me—after twenty-three years of wedded non-bliss. He was frugal, conniving, verbally abusive, and definitely had a girl friend who must have been desperate to choose him over so many others out there. But, if and when you see her, or saw her at my unveiling last year, you might understand that this old girl was not a beauty queen. So, here she is, standing at my soon to be unveiled stone with my now single and phony widowed husband, pretending to care, console, and take away some of the pain he never really felt since I passed.

I remember falling over in the kitchen, and I remember he never called 9-1-1. He waited for some reason, attempting to do chest compressions and supposedly wanting to safe my life. Yeah right! Anyone with half a brain—and his is much smaller—would know that you never move someone with a head injury…you call for help. Well, according to the rocket scientists—or EMT's and doctors—a piece of plaque broke off from my heart and blocked the oxygen from getting to my brain, causing what they claimed was my being brain dead. No one looked further, and although my sister worked hard to get many different doctors to see me—and they did—and she called every hospital in New York, Ohio, England, Germany, France, and California, no one knew what to do and no one had a solution. She even called the Kessler Foundation and the Burke Foundation, where she received some answers, but I never got there as I spent one month in ICU and then one day in Palliative Care watching Marvin wait until I expired like a parking meter.

What is going through my mind is just why he wanted me out of the way? I guess my replacement would know better than me. His family never really wanted me around, and whenever we went to his daughter's house, his ex-wife was there and they would recount their lives and their past. Just what really happened to me is still unknown. When asked, he tells the story in seven different ways. "She fell over in the kitchen washing dishes." "She fell on top of the table," explaining the black and blue mark and swollen left side of my face and forehead. "She fell when I was not in the apartment." "I was doing the laundry." I wonder if he went to do the laundry after I fell over and pretended the rest about chest compressions and more. He said, "I really can't remember; I think she was standing by the sink and fell over." "She yelled 'Help,' and fell over onto the floor." "She was walking out of the kitchen, held on to the table, and fell over." And finally, he just did not remember. But, each time he went to see me in the hospital he kept saying out loud that he felt guilty but would not say about what: you can figure that out for yourself. Each time he said it, my cousin Mara would tell him not to feel guilty, he did all he could to save me. I wonder just what her part was in all of this.

So, I am still here behind the stone, but now my mom is right next to me and she asked me to let you know that I will not give up until someone else is behind a great big stone; but not in this cemetery, and not near me. Rest comfortably while you can Marvin: You never know who is going to be the next person that is behind one of these stones. Lies, betrayals, fear...you can't escape if you are next!

Delusional: Part One

According to Wikipedia, delusions occur: Delusions typically occur in the context of neurological or mental illness, although they are not tied to any particular disease and have been found to occur in the context of many pathological states (both physical and mental). However, they are of particular diagnostic importance in psychotic disorders including schizophrenia, paraphrenia, manic episodes of bipolar disorder, and psychotic depression. Meet Ginger and you decide which disorders apply to her and just why she is delusional.

***

My name is Ginger Grace and I am behind the next big monument in this cemetery. Many of my friends cannot believe that I am gone but rest assured I am no longer among the living, but my story needs to be told. I feel that I was misunderstood, really dealt a raw deal, and what happened to me should never have happened. I speak to you from behind the last thing that someone bought for me. This monument is a tribute to me, and of course it is big, ornate, and definitely expensive. After all: I DESERVE THE BEST!

***

Why was it that everything I wanted came hard? What was wrong with this rental agent? Just because we were four months behind on our rent, did that mean they should try and evict us? Well, I wouldn't stand for that. I was sick and out of work for a while, and my boyfriend spent time in the hospital too. What were we supposed to do? I really needed that vacation, and of course the new fur jacket that kept me warm in the cold weather. I was sick and tired of seeing everyone dressed to the nines, while I had to shop in cheaper stores when I was seriously destined for better things.

Now I'd gotten a call from the ridiculous renting agent of my complex that if I didn't come up with a few thousand for the back rent I would be living in the street. They really didn't understand the struggle I had getting up in the morning just to look the right way, attempt to sell something to make a small commission, and then pick up my boyfriend from work and have dinner out. I decided to go through my phone book and hit up some people for money, and hopefully some or all would come through.

I called my boyfriend's sister and she hung up on me. How dare she say that I had borrowed my limit and never paid her back? Calling his aunt got me nowhere either. She claimed that I'd borrowed over ten thousand from her in the past, and she was not going to fork over any more money. I couldn't believe she had the audacity to tell me that I should get a real job with benefits and a real salary. I was not a well person and I could only work a certain number of hours a day.

When my dad was alive he understood my conditions and would always bail me out. Now, where was I? My mother had disowned me, but she was worthless and could not make ends meet herself. She had my grandfather to support her and buy her liquor and cigarettes. She was retired, but her pension did not cover her drinking and smoking habits, or anything else. So, what was I going to do?

I decided to rip up the notice on my door and pretend they never put it there. How could they prove that it was there? Did they photograph it? How would they know if I did that?

Next, I planned to go into the management office and tell off that witch who thought I, Ginger, would ever leave this apartment. It's not as if it was the Ritz or the Plaza. This was a middle-income complex and most of the residents thought they were well off…but just one look at them and the old-fashioned cars they drove said otherwise. At least I drove a sports car. I would never be seen in anything like a Honda or a Chevy…give me a break! So, how would I be able to cough up four thousand dollars by three that afternoon?

I could insist that my boyfriend give me money, but he claimed this was my problem and I needed to solve it myself. He could move in with his boss and ditch me at any time. After all the fun times we'd had, and the great you know what! He would never find anyone as adventurous and hot as me!

Last week when we'd walked on the beach and I was wearing my bikini, he told me that I looked like a beached whale and needed to lose weight. How wrong! I was not overweight and I was not obese. But, for some reason everyone seemed to think that I did not dress appropriately and that I looked like I weighed about 190, when I knew that I didn't. The other day I wore a really short hot pink skirt, and so many people stared at me. The women just whispered when I walked by, and I knew they were jealous.

But, getting back on track, I needed the money and I would demand that someone help me, now. But who? My ex-father in-law hung up on me. My ex-grandfather passed away before I could milk him for some money…I bet he would have taken care of me if he were still there. My boyfriend's mother helped me sometimes, but she was not there anymore either. So, what was a girl to do? Where was I going to get an advance on a job that I did not have, especially since I did not want to have to get up before noon?

Someone was at the door. Someone was *banging* on my door. I refused to answer it. They were yelling and telling me that they replaced the notice, and they knew I ripped it off the door. The marshalls were outside and they said I had until the next morning to vacate or they might arrest me. Never!

One more person to call, and she owed me big time for what I did for her. If she did not come through, I would make her pay. Could they really padlock the door so that I could not get back in once I left? How was I supposed to even attempt to get a job if I could not get back in my apartment to change, fix myself up, and get things in motion?

But, first I had to call Miranda and explain my situation. If she did not come through with the four thousand and some extra to tide me over until next month, I would reveal to her husband and family just where she went after work every day, and what she was really into.

I dialed the phone and made the call.

***

What happened? What do you think Ginger has on her friend? Where will she wind up if she gets evicted?

Delusional: Part Two

Ginger always imagines how her life would have been if someone came to her rescue and bailed her out. Ginger needs some kind of help but refuses to realize

61

that she is quite delusional, definitely a pathological liar, and a thief.

***

We bit the bullet on this one; my scheme to convince my grandfather's girlfriend to bail us out worked. The tears, the shaking, the pretend fear all worked on her. Boy, was I good! The people in the complex where I lived got paid off, but we decided to move to higher ground. I convinced her to lend us some money for a fresh start in a different community—after all, why should I have to live in a substandard home?—and before long we were married and had kids.

But why did I have to chauffeur everyone around, cook, clean, and even pick up his dry cleaning? Let his girlfriend do that for him! Having some money to play with was great, but I would have to make sure that when I spent it on myself and for my wants I still had enough to pay the rent. Unless I could convince my grandfather's girlfriend, Theresa, to hand over some more...or better yet, my dad was dating someone really rich. How about Nora? She loved me and my kids, and would never let us go hungry or get evicted.

Talking to someone in his family, I found out about money that we might inherit from his late grandfather. I was excited about the fact that we might have another windfall, if I could just convince my husband to go along with my next scheme. But, I thought we needed a new car, a vacation, and much more. I knew the rent should come first, and it would, but I really needed more than just a simple roof over my perfect head. My medical bills were piling up, and my charge cards had been suspended. I did have a day job, but I hated selling costume jewelry. Flea markets were great to make extra money, but who wanted to waste a beautiful Saturday or Sunday working when the beaches were great and the weather was perfect for tanning? My teenage daughter was working two jobs, so she could help, and my twenty-three year old son was a plumber and could afford just about anything, including helping his mother.

I had decided to contact my father-in-law and see the extent of our inheritance from my husband's grandparents. I hoped it was at least six figures. I didn't want to get short changed, and I needed to finally look at the copy of the will that I got to make sure that I got my fair share. After all, I was the one working hard to make sure that we got rich, and I was entitled to more than he was for working this deal.

I also thought I would do my best to finally take off some of my excess weight, rekindle the fires with my husband, and hopefully get rid of his manipulating girlfriend. Or, maybe I would get rid of her in another way.

One conversation can change your entire outlook. My father-in-law informed me that I was not entitled to any of the money and that all of it would go to my husband. He would make sure that I could not get my hands on any of it, and that my children and his son would be protected from my greediness and my money schemes. That's what he thought.

Life insurance was something everyone needed and should have. So, I thought a million dollar policy on my husband's life just might do the trick. Convincing him that we needed to protect each other and take out matching policies put my plan in motion. He was really stupid and never really questioned anything, thinking that he might collect on this for some reason even if I was still alive.

Now, for the master part of my master plan. I would have to wait for the policy to mature. First, I needed to do some homework, get quotes, find out the premiums, and learn the rate of return. Researching this, I learned that I needed to understand that buying a million dollar life insurance policy would provide ME with the ability to live in the lifestyle that I deserved and needed. I also learned that my goal was not for my loved ones to get rich after I passed…but then, I was going nowhere. Someone else was about to leave first. Since I had four children and my husband worked, I learned that I might need to take out a larger policy to make sure I got the maximum benefit. A million dollar policy, as far as I was concerned, was the way to go. I realized this would be expensive, but who cared? I could afford it if I could convince the dimwit to use his inheritance to pay the rent and buy this insurance for one of our futures. Plan in place, the policy was bought, and now it was time to carry out the rest.

Waiting a while before I executed the rest of my plan would require patience. In the meantime, I would have to put on a good show for everyone, even pretend to work and earn something in my menial job, and maybe make sure that the rent got paid. But, he could handle that, and I would find a way to handle some of the rest and still have time to shop, go to the spa, and relax from the hustle and bustle of life. After all, picking up the kids from school, dropping them at their friend's houses to do homework, and going out with my friends took work.

Just how was I going to execute my plan to rid myself of these burdens and finally not have to drag my body out of bed in the morning? I would have to enlist the help of someone who could get me the right poison. I needed one that would go undetected when I placed it in my husband's morning coffee.

So, just how did I wind up behind this magnificent stone? I prepared his coffee as usual. I even prepared his oatmeal the way he liked it. I guess he became suspicious because I never really did this before, but I figured he would appreciate the effort. He walked out of the dining area to get the sweetener and the cream for his coffee, and I poured the liquid poison into the black coffee. Walking back into the dining room without the sweetener, he claimed he could not find it in the cabinet. Searching through the cupboard myself, I found a box buried in the back and brought it to him. Coffee in place…. But I have more to accomplish and I am not quite done yet.

No, not dead yet. I was seriously ready for him. The end result is…well, you can guess that I collected on the policy. With him thinking that I would drink the poisoned coffee, I cleverly spilled it on the floor and asked him to pour me another. While he did that, not thinking that I was on to what he originally did, I fixed his coffee the way he liked it. You can guess the rest!

Delusional: Ginger's Fate

Sometimes people just didn't understand me. I could not figure out why they felt I was so selfish, self-absorbed, and totally unfeeling. Go figure! After all, I had a hunk for a new husband whose eyes wandered everywhere, and I had to keep track of just where they wandered to make sure they didn't permanently stray. I attempted to go to work at least twice a week to make some money to allow me to eat out with my friends, give my oldest daughter spending money, and of course pay some of the bills. My husband was too busy at the gym working out, training, and of course checking out, if you know what I mean. But, that was the least of my worries. Parents were supposed to bail out their kids when they were in trouble, but since mine were no longer available I figured I could hit my aunts, uncles, and grandfather up for some money. Why not? They all had tons and wouldn't miss a few thousand.

The landlord had called that day and told me my check for our rent bounced. I told him to redeposit the check, hoping to get the funds to cover the rent before the check bounced again. Then someone else called and said we owed him money because his check had bounced too. I hoped someone would cover the mere three hundred we owed him. If not, so what? Next, our cable and electric bills got paid, but hopefully both checks wouldn't bounce. My husband had no idea what he made in a week working, and I tried my best but I didn't think that I should have to it all by myself.

My family had given us money after the life insurance premium from my first husband's demise played out so quickly...I hadn't figured on those taxes. Of course, when my new husband's mother passed away she left us tons, but the investments I made were apparently wrong, and somehow I didn't know how all of the money was gone along with the three businesses. I thought they would do well, but as someone told me— but I did not listen—I should have looked at the demographics of the area first, checked out the traffic into the malls where the businesses were going to be, and gotten someone that understood finances to help us. But, I thought I had it under control.

Well, never mind that...I figured until everyone realized what I had done, maybe no one would get too angry and would just wait for their money. I wanted a vacation, and that came first. My daughter wanted a new car, and my other daughter needed to go to camp. So, the bills would have to go on the back burner.

I had no idea why my aunt was so mad when I asked her to pay our back rent until I caught up with our other bills. She flatly refused and told me that when she offered to get someone to handle our finances and invest the money left to us we refused to listen. It was time to grow up and take responsibility, and pay our own way.

My husband had someone giving him money and who knew what else, and was looking to move out and stick me with everything. Why should I have wound up with the three kids, the bills, having to work every day, and dealing with his problems too?

My father had always bailed me out and paid my way. Other people had too…so why not now? Why was everything my problem? I worked, but sometimes I felt that I needed a break and wanted to run away from everything. My kids needed great vacations and I did too. I needed expensive rings and clothes; and when we went to New York, why didn't any of my relatives pay for the hotel when they realized money was tight? So what if they had bills to pay too. Most of them were retired and had great pensions, and should share the wealth.

One morning I decided it was time to take matters into my own hands, so I arranged for someone to steal my car from my driveway in the middle of the night. In addition, I told someone else to break into my garage, and told the person what to steal. Why not? I had homeowner's insurance and car insurance. This would help me collect some money, and maybe pay my rent and get the creditors off of my back.

The next morning when I woke up my car was gone, and my garage looked like someone was having a rummage sale gone badly. The entire garage was ransacked and all of the power tools were gone, the bikes, the computer that I kept there, and the extra clothes for vacations. I figured the person had wanted to make it look good. Collecting from the insurance company would not be easy, but calling the police and pretending to be upset and scared that someone broke into my house was not hard. I used my acting skills, and doubted that anyone would ever think I had anything to do with this.

The police arrived and took a detailed report, and then I called my insurance company and asked that someone come out as soon as possible to assess the damage. Since things were missing from the garage, they wanted an itemized list and receipts. Trying to recall where I bought the power blower, the saw, the power tools, my extra laptop, and some old clothes that I kept in the garage, I realized that in order to collect anything major I would have to come up with items that were not in the garage and get some receipts. The car was one thing, and I knew that I would get at least book value. But, the items in the garage had to at least total three thousand dollars or my efforts would have been in vain.

My friend worked in a computer store—will not divulge the name—and I knew she would give me a receipt for the laptop and even a printer, and backdate the invoice. My other friend worked in a store like Home Depot, and she could get me receipts for the power tools, the power mower, and hopefully the rest. The clothes I had some receipts for, but the one item that I hoped I could collect on, besides the car, were the valuable baseball and football cards that were in mint condition in the trunk of the car. We had planned to take them to a collector the next day, but the car was stolen and I forgot they were there. But, how was I going to prove that I had the cards, and how would I prove their worth?

My husband was a trainer at a gym, and I was sure that if he thought really hard, which he could if he tried, he just might know someone who trained there that would vouch for us and give us a receipt, or some type of document stating the worth of the cards. But, if that did not work, I could always say that I'd had a safe in the garage that had jewelry in it. The entire garage was kept locked, so how could anyone know whether I had a safe?

Well, I bet you are wondering just how I got behind this huge stone. My husband, Jack, was a very handsome man, and most women were drawn to him at first sight. Walking into the gym in the morning he got looked at, pawed, and definitely rubbed up against by many of the women who worked and trained there. But, one was truly toxic and out for her own enjoyment, finding her way to Jack every morning, giving him more than just his schedule.

I entered the gym to bring him his cell phone that he'd left at home. Not realizing that I was there, the two of them went off to her office, never noticing that I was right behind them. I waited until they closed the door, listened for a while, and then barged in on a scene that I never expected. Needless to say I was upset, and I told this Amazon that her days were numbered in more ways than one. Things got ugly and out of control as furniture went flying, and we punched and hit each other as my husband just stood by and watched us.

But, someone called the police, and things escalated when they yelled for us to cease and desist, but neither one of us did. Then the Amazon went to her desk, pulled out a gun, and aimed it at me. At first no one could believe that she had a gun in her desk. She claimed it was for protection…from what no one really knew. But, from the phony smile on her face and the glint in her eyes, I knew that she had to have this planned. Jack had called to ask that I come to the gym with his phone so that he would know what time to pick up our middle daughter from dance class. But, in reality they had it planned. My efforts to collect some money and find a way to better our lives and finances would pay off to him and him alone.

Hoping that the police would do something and find a way to get the gun away, I moved out of her line of fire, but too late. The police fought with her to get the gun away, but it went off and got me in the chest, with a second shot in the stomach. The rest remained a blur as the ambulance came and took me to the hospital. But, I started to feel as if my body was floating, and I could see myself on the operating table with all of the doctors and nurses working hard to save my life.

When they came out and told my children that I was gone they seemed upset. My husband put on good show and lied about what really happened, and told the police that I had threatened this Amazon many times, that I'd ruined his life because of my spending, and that I had gotten what I deserved.

Well, he would never collect the insurance money because there wasn't any…I never paid the premium. He would not remain in the house because I did not pay the mortgage for five months and we were in trouble with the bank. He would never get the money for the car because it was going to be repossessed…but then, you never know, he might get lucky and get some money for the lost items that were in the garage. But, where did the money for the mortgage go? Where do you think I got the money for this great monument in this mausoleum? Lies, betrayals, deceits, and bad choices...and another incident GONE WRONG!

***

Ginger really thought that everyone should pay her way and never bothered to put aside any money for bills, her children's education, their supplies for school, or for her household expenses. Ginger asked all of her relatives for loans that she never paid back. She over extended herself with banks, and with the gyms that she bought and never paid the rent for any of them. Ginger was self centered, self-absorbed and selfish...and Ginger is behind the stone.

Appendix

"Understanding the Nature of the Truth and the Lie;
Peace and Fear,
Trust and Distrust"
By
David McDonald
&
Faith McDonald

Foreword

The following article describes the nature, principles and effects of the truth while contrasting these with the Lie and its effects, which are fear and distrust. It is set forth as an instrument of use in the holistic healing of the human psyche with a concentration placed upon that of the developing child. The ability of this instrument to accomplish this state of mental and emotional well-being relies first upon the successful illumination of its constituent parts whose careful articulation is logically stated. Secondly, for healing to occur, these concepts and principles—once understood—must be diligently applied in a consistent manner by both the individual and society as a whole.

The source of the information and viewpoints presented herein is an amalgamation of the authors' learned and experiential knowledge and that of the wisdom obtained and compiled from all the social sciences existent in their various guises. The scope of this article is confined to the description of its primary, structural components or parts with a brief description given concerning the effects of their interrelation upon American society.

By defining and understanding these parts, we shall then be able to predict the detrimental consequences upon human nature and, subsequently, society when lies are habitually used within the course of our daily interactions with one another. The illumination of the eminent harm done to both the individual and society must produce a passionate desire within us all to abandon the ills resultant from the use of the lie if ever we are to find our way to wholeness. Additionally, we must adopt the beneficial philosophy of "always telling the truth" if we are to create for ourselves an environment of openness and honesty.

We shall explore one aspect of the nature of the Truth and the nature of the Lie and that being their functions. Furthermore, it shall be shown how living the Truth brings peace and in contrast how living the Lie brings forth the emotion of fear the measurement of which is proportionate to the frequency and depth in which the lie is employed. We shall also explore certain aspects of the nature of peace and correspondingly we shall examine fear along with its alternating aggressive and debilitating effects. The causes of fear related to these aspects as well as the various remedies for it shall be explored in keeping with the scope of this article.

Finally, we shall demonstrate how a mind suspended in a state of suspicion and distrust then occurs within the individual whose environment is a construct of lies and the subsequent fears, which arise as a result of a life whose only structure is a tentative, poorly woven web of lies. We shall discuss how this suspended state of mind arrests the development of the healthy maturation of the child's mental and emotional capacities. It shall also be shown how living the Truth births peace, which in turn produces an environment of trust.

PART 1

The Nature of the Truth
Vs.
The Nature of the Lie

In beginning our study and understanding of the Truth and the Lie we use the term "nature" rather than "definition" to purport the supposition that those things called truths and lies have a rather illusive predisposition in allowing what might be considered an unambiguous description of them to ever occur. The attempted clarification of this ambiguity is not what might appear to the casual observer as a futile exercise in semantics where the scholarly sit upon imagined steeds, jousting one another with superfluous ideas. No, "the Lie" just as "the Truth" has evaded the whole of humanity's attempt to define it with all certainty from the times of antiquity even until now.

Why, we might as well describe ourselves with all certainty, mightn't we? Ah, a correlation that is not without some merit; the nature of the lie, the nature of the truth and the nature of humanity. Each remains as unfathomable and indescribable as the next and, yet, instinctively we perceive that their absolute comprehension is necessary and even vital to our personal well being. Therefore, we continue ever onward, delving into the infinite mysteries surrounding each and hoping as did our ancestors that we might avoid the endless, philosophical rhetoric and, somehow, conclusively define them.

Take heart, dear reader, for we shall avoid the endless rhetoric by avoiding that which births it—the quest for the absolute definition of the Lie, the Truth and of Ourselves. We shall instead keep our attentions focused upon the less tangible and infinitely more abstract qualities of the *nature* of these things—most particularly the nature of the Lie.

"Why must we bother with this at all?" You may ask.

Well, because we must have some working description of a truth or a lie no matter how vague it may be in order to determine if others or we are using them. Right?

However, before we discuss this nature let's first take a moment in order to illustrate how the Lie defies absolute defining and in so doing we shall imply the equally equivocally defining of the Truth. We will do this for those who believe the Lie can be described with all certainty. Let us begin with the simplest, most forthright definition and after we have disproved its usefulness, we shall proceed to the next definition and then the next and so on until we soon reach the place where you shall see that greater clarification only causes us to be unable to see the forest for the trees. In other words, all that becomes clear is that we are more confused! How about this for beginners?

The lie is any untruth: What's wrong with this? Well, to begin with you have to define the term Truth absolutely and then claim the lie to be all else. No two people have ever agreed upon a definition of "Truth" as have no two philosophies or religions. Therefore, this definition is useless without an agreed upon definition of the Truth. Secondly, to say there is only the Lie and the Truth is to claim that there are no gray areas in life; you know, places where depending on certain parameters a lie can become the truth or vice-versa or both or neither.

"How can that happen?" You ask.

Easy, say for example, I said, "I love the taste of chicken!" Then suppose I had a bad experience and ate some that was undercooked and I became very ill. Furthermore, suppose that due to this bad experience I determined to never eat it again. What if after this event I said, "I hate even the sight of chicken!"

Which then is true?

Both? Neither?

What if after both of these events I became lost in a great forest for days and days and was forced to go without anything to eat and only had some water from small streams I came across to drink? What if when I finally stumbled across some people who were camping deep in the forest I discovered that all they had to eat was chicken? Would I eat it? You had better know it—bones and all! What if after this event I said, "I like chicken, somewhat."

"Oh, come on! Make up your mind!" You shout.

So, which is true?

 The last statement?

Yes, but not until that moment and then only for that moment. At any moment afterward another event could occur which then changes my truth about the culinary acceptance of chicken. Then my truth once again becomes a lie, which may also once again be changed into the truth or something may happen to make my appetite for chicken unsettled. Sometimes I like it and sometimes I don't. No more black and white chickens for me. All my chickens are now gray. Consider this next definition:

The Lie is a misrepresentation of the facts:

Okay, but what if *I unknowingly* had my facts wrong?

"Okay then, that's easily enough fixed," you say.

The Lie is a misrepresentation of the facts done knowingly: There that seems solid! Lookout, though, here we go clarifying again! But, will our clarification endure scrutiny or simply lead to more confusion? Let's see....

What if I intended to lie, but later on the facts changed to make true what was my lie? Wouldn't that be ironic! Then I would accidentally wind up telling the truth! In the end I did just what I said I would even though it was unintentional. Would it then still be a lie? There would be no proof of wrongdoing and, therefore, nothing any system of law could denounce. I would be like those who confess to a crime where there is no proof of their wrongdoing. In such cases where there is no evidence, even a confession is not enough to convict a person, as some people have been known to confess to crimes they didn't commit.

It would then become a matter of moral judgment based upon the individual's own reasoning and belief system as to whether a lie was even told or not. It would then be a matter of individual conscience as to how much guilt should be ascribed. Some might even completely excuse themselves seeing the switch-up as being an intervention of the Fates, which kept them from any wrongdoing. Additionally, they may excuse their part in *knowingly* lying by proclaiming that "the forces that be" *did know* and superseded their authority to decide, thereby, nullifying their premeditated malicious intent. Others, however, may feel very guilty despite the turn of events being unable to consider anything but their premeditated, intended deception and declare themselves to be guilty—fully!

"How could such a situation actually happen?" You ask.

Easily actually, since we, humans, are always outsmarting ourselves causing such ironies to occur more frequently than you might suppose. But, here's just one example of how this particular switch could happen: What if I knew that a big party was going on in a college dorm across my state and I wanted to go, but had no way and, of course, couldn't ask my parents for their spare car for such a thing. To arrange it, suppose, I told my parents that a buddy of mine was in a bind and needed a ride back to his college dorm which was coincidentally just where I wanted to go anyway. Furthermore, suppose that they said, "Yes," but on the condition that I check in by phone and allow them to follow my movements by GPS.

"Fine no problem," I say smiling because I'm really going there anyway.

Then suppose that just as I am leaving I find out that a good buddy of mine actually is stranded in my town and really does need a ride back to his dorm and to the very same college the party was being held? Not only this, but I miss going to the party altogether because of the lost time it takes to help him with all his stuff. What a trip! I wound up telling the truth, but gained in the bargain another trip and one I hadn't counted on—a guilt trip for having lied to my folks.

"You didn't lie!" My buddy laughs at me on the ride over. "You didn't misrepresent the facts! You're doing just what you said you would!" he insists.

"It's still a lie because I knew it was a lie when I told it!" I object.

"No court in the world would convict you on such evidence," he laughs.

He's right, but I feel guilty anyway. You see, it's just like our chicken story. What was a lie became the truth and my initial wrong motive at best serves to only make gray the delineation of truth and lie. Are you beginning to see why the lie cannot be so easily defined, but has a nature, which must be intuitively discerned? No? Then let's do another one! What about this simple statement:

Facts don't lie: Consider these scenarios...

"Guilty!" the judge, hotly declares as he slams the gavel down.

The fact of the matter is that a court of law—an institution which we hold in the highest regard and a facet of our government in which we depend upon for justice and equity to be served—has just emphatically pronounced the defendant guilty—*that's a fact!* But, do we know for sure that the defendant is guilty? The fact is, no, we don't. We depend upon a preponderance of the evidence shown by the prosecution, whereby, all reasonable doubt of innocence has been suspended. That is, the defendant has been "proven guilty beyond a reasonable doubt."

But, reasonable doubt being established in the mind of the judge or minds of a jury by the finesse or lack thereof of the prosecution is gray at best especially when we consider the varied moral beliefs of judges and juries as they interpret the information presented to them through their own unique and often self-conflicting value system. It is why juries often find a defendant innocent when popular public opinion was guilty, or vice-versa, and why at times "hung juries" occur, which means they were unable to reach a unanimous decision.

Here's another scenario where facts have been proven to lie:

The Christian belief system is based upon faith. What this means is that those who believe in the goodness, mercy and promises of God can pray and ask him to change facts about their lives, which are undesirable. For example, doctors may diagnose a patient with Cancer and will only do so after they have thoroughly established this as a fact. The Christian then has a choice to accept this diagnosis, which is a fact as being truth, or to refute it. To do so the Christian must ask God for healing in the name of Jesus and then believe by faith that they then receive it—that is, at the time of asking for it. They must believe they are *already* healed before any facts change to support such a belief. That's how it is of faith—because it is believed to be received before it is seen as a fact. The Bible calls this, "Speaking those things that be not as though they are."

To many this would be lying, but to the Christian it is the way to change the facts of this life into the blessings of God. Many a doctor have scratched their heads in disbelief as a patient—who was formerly and of a fact chronically ill—is suddenly and miraculously made whole and well without the remedies of modern medicine. Christians may go about confessing all kinds of things that line themselves up with what the Word of God says concerning them and not with what the facts say. Some examples are, "By his stripes, I am healed; Let the weak say I am strong and let the poor say I am rich; I am the head and not the tail; I am above and not beneath."

As a matter of fact, according to the Bible, there is nothing that a Christian can receive from God that is not by faith. So, all that the Christian beholds that is not as God says it should be is perceived as a lie. Ask a Christian the facts that he or she has seen God change for them, as they believed by faith God's promises. It is a kind of thinking that may open a completely different world to you. At the very least, you will see the complexities of defining what is truth, and what is a lie.

If after considering these examples you are thoroughly confused about what is truth and what is a lie then you are just where everybody else has been who has set out to define either. Now, we are positioned to embrace understanding the concept of the *Nature of the Lie* and, conversely, the *Nature of the Truth*, which is the only real way to tell the difference between the two and, *YES*, there is a difference!

Let's begin by describing what we mean by the term "nature." We use this term to describe a set of thoughts, words, and behaviors, which may be attributed or associated with the Lie, which distinguish it from a mutually exclusive set belonging to the truth. Each set may be clinically described in so much that they are free of judgment, values, or reason. It is when we apply judgment, values and reason to interpreting these behaviors that we enter into the before experienced realm of confusion where philosophers, poets and lawyers abide. Notice how much clearer the distinction between truth and the lie grows as we constrain ourselves to simply noting its nature.

Okay, in keeping with the limited scope of this article, we shall confine our discussion of the primary or principle parts of the nature of the Truth and the Lie to

85

their functions as was mentioned in the Foreword. To begin with, what do we mean by a function? In this context, function means the purposes for which both the Truth and the Lie were and are brought into existence or the effect(s) each causes. Simple enough, huh? Yep! So, let's start describing—not defining—the functions both of the Truth and of the Lie:

There are three distinct functions, which we shall talk about concerning both the Truth and the Lie. I want you to notice throughout how that the statements concerning the Truth are statements of "being" (i.e. they are non-reactionary being free of any agenda other than to be). This does not mean they are without purpose. The Truth has purposes, but establishes and accomplishes them whether the Lie exists or not. This is not so for the Lie whose functions are clearly seen to be reactions to the Truth which are meant to destroy it, as are their observable agendas or purposes for why they exist. The Truth, however, must have the innate capacity to cleanse itself from the Lie and its effects if it is to remain the Truth. The Truth accomplishes this "healing" of itself much as the immune system of the human body protects and purges itself from disease.

Let's begin by stating as simply as possible our first, observable function of the Truth:

THE TRUTH IS A STATEMENT(S) WHICH ACCURATELY DESCRIBES IN A TIME-DEPENDENT MANNER THE STRUCTURES OF ANY OR ALL COMPONENTS IN EXISTENCE ALONG WITH THEIR RELATIONSHIPS, PROCESSES, AND EFFECTS.

Conversely, we may state our first, observable function of the Lie: THE LIE IS A STATEMENT(S) BROUGHT INTO EXISTENCE TO CONCEAL, HIDE OR TWIST THE TRUTH. Notice how that we are neither judging nor placing values upon either actions, but are simply stating them as being observable, functional traits of the nature of the Truth and of the Lie, respectively. In keeping with accordance of the principle of the scientific experiment, these functions are observable and repeatable and their effects, therefore, are predictable. See, how simple and distinguishable the Truth and the Lie have suddenly become?

What things does the Lie wish to conceal (i. e. put in an open, but unapparent place) or hide   (i. e. put in a secret, hard to discover place) and what things does the Lie wish to twist or wick (i.e. to slightly deviate from the original so as to avoid detection) from its true nature?

The answer is the very things we just mentioned in our description of the term, "nature." Remember, we said, "we use this term to describe a set of thoughts, words, and behaviors which may be attributed or associated with the Lie which distinguishes it from a mutually exclusive set belonging to the truth." So, the Lie is brought into existence to conceal, hide, or twist thoughts, words and behaviors associated with the Truth.

Why would we, humans, want to do such things?

The answer has nothing to do with understanding the simplistic function we have just revealed about the

Lie. No, the answer to that question has to do with something else entirely and that is the description of human nature, which we also promised to discuss briefly in the Foreword. So, since it's come up let's talk a minute about the part of human nature which lend itself to this first function of the Lie. But, as we do so, please keep in mind that we are talking about two different things—the nature of the Lie and Human Nature.

With this in mind, why would we want to bring a lie into existence in order to conceal or hide our thoughts, words, or behaviors? I'm sure you have answers ready enough, but if not here are just a few generalities, which are all that is needed to make the point. First, we may want something or think of something, which we believe if others knew of it, they would in all likelihood disapprove. Or, we may say something which we later regret and wished we hadn't because of the damage it caused. Therefore, we claim we said something else or meant something else by what we said other than what was understood. Therefore, we see right away that the approval of others is of the utmost importance to us.

Such approval often times goes far beyond the receiving of any vainglory and is, in fact, necessary for the well-being of any person. Moreover, the well-being of any life may be measured in how well that life is socially connected. A person who is socially well connected has been careful to forge quality relationships with people of integrity. It follows that it takes a person of integrity to hold such relationships. As goes the saying, "It's not *what* you know, but *who* you know that matters." This statement is a hyperbole in that it minimizes the importance of gaining knowledge and skills in order to make the point more fully that "knowing the right people" is vital also.

Finally, we may actually do something that is socially unacceptable and thus bring a lie into existence in order to hide our actions and, thereby, avoid the consequences. Similarly, we make subtle modifications in the Truth (i.e. twist or wick) in order to make ourselves look better or others worse. Or, we twist the Truth for some type of personal gain such as wealth, prestige or position. The list of motivations for "wicking" (i.e. as the wick of a candle is made by twisting two separate wicks into a single one) the Truth are without number. It is noteworthy that the Lie may be fabricated before the event in order to establish an alibi. This is often the case when a course of premeditated events is deemed necessary.

We may now state the second behavioral observation of the nature of the Truth—THE TRUTH REVEALS OR MAKES KNOWN THE CONDITION OF ANY OR ALL COMPONENTS IN EXISTENCE RELATIVE TO A POINT IN TIME. Again, this statement is an observable, repeatable and, therefore, predictable behavioral trait of the truth that is free of any interpretation or assigned values. Notice the word "condition" in the above statement. Condition refers to the degree to which the Truth has been left pure or the degree to which it has been wicked by the Lie.

Relative to a given point in time it is conceivable that the Lie may cease to exist entirely or, conversely, so might the Truth. In addition, the Truth may exist along side of the Lie as might parallel realities or universes, but they are never cohabitants as a little of the Lie makes the Truth a lie. The Truth, by its very nature, tends to purify itself from the wicking of the Lie. Thus, the Truth corrupted by the Lie and made a lie is able through the virtue inherent within it to become the Truth again. So is its nature.

Now, we are ready to describe the second function of the nature of the Lie—THE LIE IS BROUGHT INTO EXISTENCE TO OBSCURE OR NULLIFY THE TRUTH CONCERNING ANY OR ALL COMPONENTS IN EXISTENCE. Again, notice how we are neither judging nor placing a value upon this action, but are simply stating it as an observable behavioral trait of the nature of the Lie. Inherent in the second function of the Lie is the axiom that the Truth is in existence before the Lie and that the Lie is in effect an attack upon the Truth in order to pollute, twist or wick its nature. This behavioral observation of the Lie is consistent also with its first function, which we have described.

The third function of the nature of the Truth is— AT SOME POINT IN TIME THE TRUTH ESTABLISHES THAT WHICH SHALL ALWAYS BE FOR A GIVEN COMPONENT. Inherent in this statement is the axiom that the Truth is first established, that it wars and purifies itself from the Lie (as stated in the second function of the Truth) and continues onward everlastingly establishing conditions, which shall forever be. The Truth eliminates the existence of the Lie through the act of being the Truth. Again, this statement is an observable, repeatable and, therefore, predictable behavioral trait of the truth, which is free of any interpretation or assigned values.

One has only to consider the subject of history in any discipline to prove the point. The beginning truth is that which actually occurred. The lie is the polluted truth recorded and the established truth is the truth that shall ever be—the truth which is purified through discovery. This established truth is the truth we are forever seeking when we revisit our history books and make them clean and free of untruths and prejudiced or biased remarks. We find these eternal truths when we reassess our scientific theories and bring them more into line with fresh evidence, which we have discovered or unearth.

Additionally, we discover the truth about ourselves as we delve further and further into our own nature. We do so in order to discover our essence and why it is we do the things that we do and this so that we might bring about changes, which create greater peace and harmony in the world. All that we do is a quest for the Truth—a truth free of any pollutants and one, which establishes those things that shall forever be. It is notable that human nature tends toward discovering and establishing the truth.

We are now ready to describe the final function of the nature of the Lie—THE LIE IS BROUGHT INTO EXISTENCE IN ORDER TO CONSTRUCT A FALSE

REALITY. We may define "false reality" as any construct of the world and the things in it, which has little or no validation with the perceptions, beliefs, history, and projected future of humankind as a whole. If a life becomes for the most part constructed of lies then, subsequently, it forms a reality for the individual (or small group) which is alienated and dysfunctional since it is in opposition to the flow of ideas and actions of mainstream humanity. An individual who holds fast to this personal (or small group), artificial construct of reality is often exhibiting some form of mental illness such as schizophrenia.

In the case of a small group, the causation of the individual's frame of mind may be something other than mental illness. Leaders of such small groups may employ a method known as "brainwashing" in order to procure their absolute adherence and devotion to the group's ideas and purposes. This is where the minds of their members are reprogrammed (i.e. given a different set of priorities, values, goals, and cognitive/subconscious mental processes). It may even be that those who lead the group do not believe in the ideas they forcefully impose upon their members, but use them, rather, as a mechanism to bring about unreasonable zealotry or devotion of their followers which unbeknownst to them will achieve their leaders' own, unrevealed schemes.

The methods of brainwashing are varied, but the object is always to establish in the recipient's mind a belief in a false reality— either which was, is, or is to come. This false reality is impressed upon the person through repetitively enforced and often violent enough methods to induce a state of trauma. In this state of trauma, the ideas are embedded with fear and, therefore, carry a "charged" or more powerful condition than other ideas as they are linked to perceptions of protection and survival. These super-charged thoughts and memories over-ride other cognitive processes and cause the individual to react instinctively upon the "programming" instead of being able to think and act rationally.

This repetitive enforcement of forced ideas can in-and-of-itself be considered violent. It is interesting to note that the violence may only be implied. For example, a threat of harm may be perceived as to what the group may do if compliance to their wishes is not made. Alternatively, a state of trauma may be achieved by the group's stating what dangers the world holds for them if compliance is not made so as to gain safety from the group. If the idea is enforced enough its perceived danger becomes as great as any realized danger. This final function of the Lie serves to destroy the mental and emotional well-being of the individual (or small group) and to alienate them from most of society.

We restate our principles of the nature of the Truth here so that one may plainly see the logical and progressive nature of the stated functions of the Truth as it purges itself of the Lie and establishes an everlasting reality free of corruption:

THE TRUTH IS A STATEMENT(S) WHICH ACCURATELY DESCRIBES IN A TIME-

DEPENDENT MANNER THE STRUCTURES OF ANY OR ALL COMPONENTS IN EXISTENCE ALONG WITH THEIR RELATIONSHIPS, PROCESSES, AND EFFECTS.

THE TRUTH REVEALS OR MAKES KNOWN THE CONDITION OF ANY OR ALL COMPONENTS IN EXISTENCE RELATIVE TO A POINT IN TIME.

AT SOME POINT IN TIME, THE TRUTH ESTABLISHES THAT WHICH SHALL ALWAYS BE FOR A GIVEN COMPONENT.

Also, in restating the principles describing the nature of the Lie one can plainly see the logically progressive nature of the stated functions of the Lie as it wars against the Truth in an attempt to create a false and impossible reality:

THE LIE IS A STATEMENT OR COLLECTION OF STATEMENTS BROUGHT INTO EXISTENCE TO CONCEAL, HIDE OR TWIST THE TRUTH.

THE LIE IS BROUGHT INTO EXISTENCE TO OBSCURE OR NULLIFY THE TRUTH.

THE LIE IS BROUGHT INTO EXISTENCE IN ORDER TO CONSTRUCT A FALSE REALITY.

These statements and their preceding explanations describing both the nature of the Truth and of the Lie are superior tools we may use in differentiating between what is the Truth and what is the Lie. Absolute defining of either the Truth or the Lie is an elusive, exasperating exercise in futility as was demonstrated earlier with our use of examples near the beginning of Part One. These combined six principles of the functions and nature of the Truth and the Lie are also restated here so that you may go back to the examples given where an absolute defining was sought and see how when applied they are able to remove all confusion and easily discern between what is the Truth and what is the Lie.

PART 2

Fear,
Child of the Lie;
Peace,
Child of the Truth

In beginning our exploration of Fear (the result or child, so to speak, of fear) we must further examine that which gives fear—or peace for that matter—strength and that is *Faith.* Earlier, we discussed the faith that a Christian must use in order to access God's promises. Now, however, we shall show how all the world and every person in it is forced to use faith in the course of their daily lives from the simplest of thoughts and behaviors to the most complex. That's right, faith is used by all and not just by the religious. Moreover, depending on whether one's faith is placed in the Truth or the Lie shall determine which child is birthed—peace or fear. After we discuss faith and its relation to the Lie we shall see how Fear is the child of the Lie. Correspondingly, we shall do the same for the Truth and its child, Peace.

Can you imagine how impossible it would be to make any plans for the future if you didn't know you were going to be alive to carry out such plans? Of course, that's just how it is; none of us do know if we shall be alive even in the next moment, much less for an extended block of time stretching into the future. In this uncertain age, death comes not only in all its usual ways, (i.e. accidents, diseases, genetic anomalies which give rise to health conditions that are life threatening and homicide) but in the newest fashion—at least for Americans—terrorism which may be classified as war or mass murder.

Since our continued existence is so tentative, how is it that we are able to rationally go forward and live our lives as if we are guaranteed even reasonable longevity? The answer is faith. Furthermore, if we live life fully then that shows we have faith that good things by-in-large will happen to us and for us. If, however, we allow ourselves to believe that only harm will happen to us and that none of our dreams have any hopes of fruition then we are allowing fear to live in us by believing in a hopeless future. The nature of Truth is to build, so if we base our lives upon truth then we may expect our lives to be built up. The nature of the Lie is to tear down or destroy and, so, if we are employing the Lie in our lives then we may expect destructive, negative things to occur. It is only reasonable.

So then, what might be some examples to prove that all must live by faith? Let's begin with just what we think. In our minds, we are constantly running mock scenarios where an imagined environment relative to some concern or desire we have is conceived. In this imagined world we play the "what if" game. The object of the game is to follow a chain of reasoned events for each scenario and then choose the scenario, which seems the most probable. This is a kind of war-game we have acquired as an adaptive skill of survival and its use is also common in business. It may prove beneficial to us by allowing us to be one-step ahead of eminent danger. But, what if we're wrong? As it turns out, we are most of the time and so, all we got for all the mental exercise is unnecessary anxiety.

You've probably heard of Agoraphobia—which is an abnormal fear of being in open or public places. Agoraphobics find it very difficult to leave the perceived safety of their home. What might the thoughts be of an agoraphobic person? *Pain, harm and/or death await me outside that door,* is the sum of all the mock scenarios they run in their minds. There is no situation imagined which is perceived as having a probable or even possibly positive outcome. *Nothing out there is worth the danger that awaits!* Is this a rationale state of mind? That is, do the perceived threats correlate in any wise with the actual or probable threats which statistically may be proven? The answer is, "No."

In, fact, look at the data below where the top ten killers for the U. S. are listed. As you, do so remember what we learned earlier about facts and the Truth.

Statistical data is, however, among the most reliable kinds of fact; although, their misinterpretation is notorious. Based upon these facts you'll notice that all of those dangers listed can get to you in the supposed safety of your home:

Number of Deaths for Leading Causes of Death in U. S. per Year

1. Heart disease: 597,689
2. Cancer: 574,743
3. Chronic lower respiratory diseases: 138,080
4. Stroke (cerebrovascular diseases): 129,476
5. Accidents (unintentional injuries): 120,859
6. Alzheimer's disease: 83,494
7. Diabetes: 69,071
8. Nephritis, nephrotic syndrome, and nephrosis: 50,476
9. Influenza and Pneumonia: 50,097
10. Intentional self-harm (suicide): 38,364

Turns out, the home is not so safe after all—not to mention a recent increase in the number of home invasions. Do you see how each of us who leaves his or her home must do so with the belief or faith that we are assured relative safety while out? Or, that we may leave our home and go about our business in the world and return with all probability to its imagined safety? The difference between the Agoraphobic and the Non-

Agoraphobic could be faith in the validity of these statistics or it may be faith in the continuance of either the good or the bad experiences each has had while away from the home. Or, the dangers—supposed or real—could be all in the mind of either as well.

But, understand that though all faith is blind in that it winks at certain facts or logic, each kind also has a rationale or philosophy upon which its believers base their faith; to the Muslim it's the Koran; to the Christian, the Bible; to the scientist it is faith in what he or she can discover and claim as the truth—a theory which is a concept about the structure and function of the universe and those things in it which has yet to be disproved. Therefore, in order for it to be faith it must be faith in something even if it is no more than faith in one's own personal philosophy about the world. So, even though all faith is based upon some rationale or philosophy, it must at some point escape the restrictions of that rationale and operate where only it can—in a realm where believers, by faith, conduct their lives expecting the occurrence of events which might be considered unlikely or even impossible by those of having different faiths.

Another example of faith in our thought life that is used by the non-religious or secular world is the stock market. Shares or small pieces of ownership in corporations along with commodities like silver, gold and wheat and financial instruments such as T-Bills, bonds, money markets, and futures are traded at exchanges like the New York Stock Exchange, the S& P and the NASDAQ. Shareholders buy or sell their

101

shares and/or financial instruments and commodities based on whether they BELIEVE the price of whatever they are holding will go up or down. If they believe it will go down (i.e. the paid more for it they can get and so would be losing money) they will sell. If, however, they believe it will go up then they will buy it quick and then sell it when they think it has reached the height of its climb. Based on the most up-to-date information, complex formulas and "gut feelings" they speculate on which way they believe the price will go and then take the leap of faith and jump!

Is the stock market really something done by faith? You had better know it is! It is, because it is speculation about future events based not only upon "solid" information, (i.e. new product innovation, a company's financial statements, government policies, shift in a company's owners or management, supply and demand perceptions, conditions of overseas governments, economies and markets just to name a few) but on gut feelings, desires, hopes, dreams and last, but not least— either fear or peace.

If people who are trading in and influencing the stock market have a pessimistic view of the economy then their belief that things are bad and are getting worse will negatively affect the market as they trade off their company shares and choose what they consider to be "safer investments," which action often times tend to stagnate money and product flow. Through their faith they actually facilitate what they believed would happen. Wall Street's panicky nature is legendary as is their ability to produce the very results their fears forecast.

Other than our thoughts, we must also live by faith when it comes to our words. Have you ever thought about how much we depend upon one another to communicate effectively and keep our promises so that our lives can assume circuits of health and normalcy? The recipe for disaster is no mystery. First, you "knead" a pound of promises; next you let it "lie" before throwing in a pinch of clarification and a dash of confusion. In other words, promises are made, but not kept and possibly were never planned on being kept. Let's look at the mindset of the management of an unscrupulous or at least inefficient company.

It actually goes down like this...You place your order with the cheerful salesperson being careful to articulate every detail accurately so that there can be no confusion. You hang up the phone, pleased with yourself and confident in the good ole American machine of commerce. A couple of days later you discover from your bank that you've been charged more for the product than you were expecting. After a phone call to the company, you successfully extract an explanation—albeit confused—for the extra cost, but no refund.

Two weeks later (later than the cheery, salesperson promised and after several more, less-than-cheery interactions with the company) your long awaited package arrives. You eagerly tear into it for the much wanted and long awaited item only to discover that they have sent you the wrong product! It's the cheaper, look-a-like item you were so careful to clarify from the one you wanted in your initial phone call when you painstakingly made clear your order. You lick your wounds and find what solace you can by submitting a scathing report of the incident to the BBB.

Can you see how telling lies, one to another, destroys our faith in the integrity and work ethics of the American machine of commerce? Sure, and yet we must continue onward being a little wiser and, hopefully, not jaded being cleansed from any bitterness of heart by belief in the Truth that people are—by in large—good and companies are—by in large—run efficiently; that there are more positive experiences in life than negative and that your peace is something that is worth holding onto even if it makes no sense. Peace is the effect achieved upon the mind when one is persuaded by faith that life is good and is filled with far more beneficial occurrences than harmful ones. Fear is the effect achieved upon the mind when one is persuaded by faith that life is a death sentence and people are the executioners.

PART 3

Lies + Fear = Distrust
Truth + Peace = Trust

Peace and fear are not the end of our equation as you will soon see. Part 3 describes the environment of one's life and the continued state of mind that comes to settle upon those who choose to have faith either in the Truth or in the Lie. In this section we shall show how living in and using lies not only births fear, but constructs an unhealthy environment in which to live and a correspondingly detrimental state of both the conscious and subconscious mind. Furthermore, we shall see that distrust and its accompanying apprehensions paralyze and inhibit the healthy development and expression of the mind.

In contrast, we shall, also, see how a life lived in the Truth not only births peace of mind, but produces also an environment of trust and security where in one may live, thus allowing a healthy development of the mind. The expansive expression of a healthy mind heals not only the life of one blessed with such a mind, but is an agent for healing in the lives of all those that it may effectively reach. Truth is not bound within the hearts of those who know it, but as its nature is to heal and cleanse itself from the Lie so it accomplishes this in the lives of others when it is deposited into their own hearts and minds. Regrettably, the Lie through its birthing of fear is able to accomplish the reverse with equal intensity.

Okay, let's first look at how Lies + Fear = Distrust. Again, a couple of simple examples may go far in illustrating the point. Suppose you told a female friend of yours that, a mutual girlfriend was saying hurtful things about her behind her back. It isn't true and you have said it because you fear that you are beginning to lose your position as the primary friend among the three. You don't like how chummy your two girlfriends have become with one another of late and so you've decided to drive a bit of a wedge between them. You have damage control planned, though, as you don't want your friends to become enemies. Now, this is the scenario and we will see in a moment how it plays out, but let's hold on and look at something else before we proceed.

Before this lie, there is actually another lie, which, though not spoken, has been believed. By whom? By you! You see the lie is that your two girlfriends have become closer friends of late. The truth actually is that nothing has changed. What happened? You misread and misinterpreted things that were said and done to come to this erroneous conclusion. Things are just as they were and you are still number one, but maybe not for long because now you have set out to fix something that wasn't broken and all because you feared to lose your power position. Can you see how the lie—though just a misconception, but one you believed to be true—birthed fear in you and now your mindset is one of distrust? Yep, these misconceptions happen all the time and when they do fear, and distrust inevitably follow.

Okay, let's get back to your grand scheme and see how that works out. Now, we're at the point to where you have told one girlfriend that the other has said hurtful things about her. Of course, she is initially hurt, but then becomes angry and is ready to confront her soon to be ex-friend. Now, comes the part of your grand scheme where you apply damage control and re-establish yourself as number one.

"No, no, don't do that," you insist. "Let me talk to her and I'll get to the bottom of it."

Well, your friend is okay with that and you leave in the guise of peacemaker go right off to confront the supposed malicious friend.

"What!" she screams after hearing some of the things that she supposedly said about her good friend. "I would never say such things about her!" she declares obviously hurt.

"I didn't think you would," you assure her. "Listen, I'm going to get this straightened out. I'll tell her you never said such things and she had better believe me. But, let's never talk of this again and don't you ever mention it to her. It will only cause trouble. Just drop it, okay?"

"Okay," your friend agrees and the thanks you for fixing it.

Returning to your other friend you let her know that you had a long talk with your mutual friend and come to find out she never said those things. As a matter of fact she was just repeating what someone else had said, but had added how it couldn't possibly be true.

"That's a relief," your friend says with a smile. "I didn't think she would say those things about me."

"Yep, just a big misunderstanding," you agree smiling. "But listen," you whisper. "Please, don't say anything about this to her. It will just cause problems."

"Okay," she agrees.

But, unknown to you she read something in your tone which didn't settle well with her; something which she determines to find out about.

You, however, finish your dirty business quite proud of yourself and your acute understanding of human nature. These are your thoughts, *Even though they are friends again there will remain a little hurt between them and fear that that hurt might occur again. From this point, they won't know for sure if the other is lying to them or telling the truth. There will be distrust between them.* Now, watch as the Truth purifies itself from the Lie.

Your friend who picked up on your suspicious tone had a talk with your mutual friend—a long talk. They worked through it until the Truth stood up bold and proud. They decided on a course of action, which would empower them and remove your persuasive influence. Yep, your girlfriends told everybody what you did—the truth, the whole truth and nothing but the truth. Now, you can't buy a friend. People fear you because of your lies recognizing that you through those lies tried to destroy lives. Now, no one trust you and you project your anger from being shunned upon all believing yet another lie and so fear and distrust all. Do you see how the actions can potentially damage the emotional development of all those involved?

While some people who hear about the incident take it as a warning to trust no one others who hear of the two girls honesty have renewed faith in humanity and are able to trust more. Do you see how the beliefs and actions of these three girlfriends had a ripple effect creating an increase of trust and a decrease of distrust in one segment—those who believe in the Truth? On the other hand, we can see an increase in distrust and a decrease in trust in that segment of the population, which believed the Lie or the pessimistic, negative viewpoint of human nature. In this group, healthy development has been damaged.

In the end that's what is is—a choice as to which one you will believe and it is according to each person's make-up and personality as to which they will decide to believe. Each shall then employ the mechanism of faith of which we describe earlier; mechanisms that supersede the facts and come to a conclusion which is made outside of the knowledge provided by the facts. Each segment of people shall believe in the Truth or the

Lie according to a philosophy of life they are either developing or have already developed.

Let's look at one more example of how Lies + Fear = Distrust. Suppose a stock broker is in a position to make a "killing" in the market through some information he had inadvertently and innocently come across—information considered "insider information" by the SEC and, therefore, unlawful for use by any dealing in market trade. Further, suppose that this broker is already in a bind having not made many wise investments of late which has his firm and his clients quite upset. Always having been the type of person to play by the rules, he has in the past, refused such dark opportunities even though he has seen his colleagues get away with similar actions, prosper, and be promoted. Recently, however, he has begun to question the "good guy" philosophy and is beginning to think that the old adage, *Good guys always finish last,* may be true after all.

This is our scenario, but as with our previous example, let's consider the unspoken lie(s) that have been believed by our broker to provoke him into the illegal activity in which he is about to engage. If we will recall our statements of the nature of the Truth, we remember that it shall always purify itself from the Lie and make itself known to all. Therefore, there is nothing covered that shall not be revealed—sooner or later. Every wrong doer innately knows this and it is why he or she sleep with one eye open and are always looking over their shoulder for the day when their deceit shall be discovered and it will be time to pay for the crime. This is the first, unspoken Lie our broker has believed—*I can get away with it.*

Another unspoken lie believed by our broker is a misconception that the old adage, *good guys always finish last,* is a negative statement and, therefore, an undesirable way to be. A corollary of this statement is, *there are no shortcuts in life.* Good guys may finish last, but at least they finish! Bad guys *and gals* look for shortcuts or easy ways to make-it in life and most often wind up in jail and as a result are usually unable to finish what they were doing. Such shortcuts are most always illegal or at least immoral; otherwise, they would be mainstream methods of conducting business or one's life. Have you ever been in a car with someone "who knew a short-cut?" That's right, you both get lost and instead of saving time you lose it and may never even get to where you were going.

There are other unspoken lies believed by our hapless broker, which have provoked him into taking the wrong path in life, but these suffice to make the point. Now, let's get on with our hypothetical story so that we can see how Lies + Fear = Distrust. Suppose that on top of everything else that's going wrong in our broker's life that he suddenly begins to pass kidney stones. He rushes to the E. R. where his vitals are taken and he is then taken to an E. R. partitioned room (i.e. the kind separated only by curtains from the other patients). There while waiting to be attended an extraordinary thing happens...

A man having a heart attack is brought to the curtained room right next to our broker's little room. Of course, everyone forgets about him not only because a heart attack takes precedence over kidney stones, but because of who the man is. Our broker pays little attention to anything but his own excruciating misery until he hears the man's name. It is a well-known name throughout the world and one of prominence in the communication software industry.

It can't be him, he thinks.

He can't help but hear what's going on next to him. After only a few more moments, it becomes clear that the man is indeed the ingenious designer of the most used software among portable communication devices in the world and is C. E. O. of the giant corporation, which holds the lion's share of sales in the computer and communication industry. This man is perceived to be more than the head of the company; he is the heart and soul, the vision and drive of the company—*why he is the company and without him, there is no company!*

After some time, he hears the doctor tell the esteemed patient that preliminary tests show blockage in two arteries, but that they are in good places where stints may be easily inserted and that there is no reason to believe that he shouldn't recover fully and be better than ever in a couple of days. Our broker decides then and there to move over to the dark side. His first action is to leave the hospital having received no treatment and much to the displeasure of one nurse in particular who went out of her way to document his abrupt departure.

His second action is to convince all his clients who hold shares in the esteemed patient's company or companies, which are connected to his to sell their shares and to buy in the leading competitor's corporation. This they do, though, after more than a little coaxing. Our wayward broker then calls the biggest newspapers—anonymously, of course—and tells them of the "massive heart attack" suffered by the communication industry giant. The paper then verifies through their "sources" that the Big Man has indeed suffered a heart attack, though its severity is not known. Nevertheless, "massive heart attack" sells the most papers and so that is what they go with and print. Before dawn, the news is out and the stock price of the biggest computer and communication products corporation has sharply declined.

Our wily broker then watches the price of the stock fall throughout the day waiting until it reaches what he considers to be the lowest point it will go before it is found out and reported that the heart attack was minor in nature. He knows those who direct the corporation will want to get the truth out ASAP so as to stop the damage being done to the company and its interests. He smells a statement as to the well-being of the C. E. O. soon to be announced. Feverishly, he then calls all those whom he had convinced to sell and has them buy back their shares and then some as he expects the firms common stock value to climb above where it was once people find out the Big Man is actually in better health now than before.

What happens? Why, our hapless broker gets filthy rich over night, as do all those who followed his advice. He is promoted and hailed as the new wizard of Wall Street. Heck, his wife even says, "I love you, darling," again. The giant corporation isn't harmed and in fact is doing better than ever. Even the competition is able to hold on to some of the clients that made the switch during the sell off and buy back frenzy. It seems all have come out winners making our broker everyone's hero; everyone's, but one, that is...the Truth. Lookout, here comes it nature...being itself purifying itself and establishing that which shall always be.

Remember, the hurried exit our broker made from the hospital? Incidentally, he passed the stones on his own the day he was waiting for the stock price to hit bottom being so caught up in the excitement of becoming an over-night sensation that he was hardly aware of the pain. Anyway, you may recall mention of a somewhat annoyed nurse who took it upon herself to document our broker's hasty retreat. This same nurse was aware of the esteemed C. E. O.'s visit to the E. R. as she was that our broker was in the curtained room next to him, though, she couldn't know then he was a broker. Also, she had read of the misreports of a "massive heart attack" in the paper and had seen the ensuing drop in the corporation's stock price.

The next morning the paper had corrected the report to what the truth about the severity of the heart attack actually had been. Stock prices for the corporation were shown in the paper to have risen to new highs and there was something else in the paper, which caught the eye of the vigilant nurse. It was a picture of a man who seemed to foresee it all and, consequently, had become the new darling of Wall Street. Of course, our dutiful nurse recognized our hapless broker from his grinning picture in the paper and proceeded to make a few calls of her own.

The broker's picture remained on the news for several days as did the fact that the SEC was investigating the firm for which the broker worked as well as certain other individuals who had made a "killing" by following the broker's advice. As it turns out, he was forced to tell many what he had overheard in order to get them to go along with it. Well, the Truth being what she is revealed just who those certain people were and they are now in the same "country club" for white-collar criminals as is our hapless broker.

The damage done can be seen as reaching beyond that of those directly involved in this plot to gain wealth in a fashion society has deemed illegal. If one chooses, he or she might conclude that because of this incidence that, *no one can be trusted!* That *the newspapers always print the sensational and not the truth!* That, *Wall Street is full of crooks!* To do so, though, takes a certain negative mind-set—Distrust—which is itself the product of Lies and Fear.

There is an entirely different way, however, which these events might be interpreted if faith in the Truth instead of the Lie is used. One could say, "the benefit achieved can be seen as reaching far beyond the effect of isolating from society those directly involved in this plot to gain wealth. Indeed, we believe that in the long run it may even benefit them by causing them to be citizens of integrity. Furthermore, it has shown that all wrongs are eventually made right and gives us confidence to know our system works and that there are people out there (like our nurse) who as voices of the Truth make sure that Truth ever prevails.

"Life imitates art," is another saying. People ascribe various interpretations to the meaning of this enigmatic proverb. One of the more common interpretations is that we actually determine what is in the world by first conceiving it within our minds and then producing or creating that something (art) so then that artful thing then becomes a part of our lives and the world around us. Life—those thing in the world of our lives—comes from art—the mind and imagination of us all. The Truth and the Lie may well be considered art in their own rights. Certainly, it is true that our lives are an imitation of the truth, peace and trust that resides within the hearts of those so inclined as it is, also, an imitation of the lies, fear and distrust residing in the hearts of those that are so disposed.

Which is right and good or which is evil?

That which builds us up and does not destroy us...that which builds an environment of trust and not an environment of suspicion and distrust...that which causes us to see our fellow human-being as a friend and not an enemy—that.

ABOUT THE AUTHOR

Fran Lewis: Fran worked in the NYC Public Schools as the Reading and Writing Staff Developer for over 36 years. She has three masters Degrees and a PD in Supervision and Administration. Currently, she is a member of Who's Who of America's Teachers and Who's Who of America's Executives from Cambridge. In addition, she is the author of three children's books and a fourth that has just been published on Alzheimer's disease in order to honor her mom and help create more awareness for a cure. The title of my new Alzheimer's book is Memories are Precious: Alzheimer's Journey; Ruth's story and Sharp as a Tack and Scrambled Eggs Which Describes Your Brain? Fran is also the author of Faces Behind the Stones, Bad Choices and M.J. Magazine an E-Magazine dedicated to the memory of her sister Marcia Joyce. She is also a member of Continental's Who's Who of America's Executives and Professionals and the author of 11 titles. She is presently working on creating a second radio show called Chat Time with Fran Lewis on Blog Talk Radio the Red River Network and adding more outstanding shows on the World of Ink

Network. Her show Book Discussion is heard all over the world and she has many listeners.

She was the musical director for shows in her school and ran the school's newspaper. Fran writes reviews for authors upon request and for several other sites. You can read some of my reviews on Ezine.comand on ijustfinished.com under the name Gabina. Here is the link to her radio show **www.blogtalkradio.com**

Made in the USA
Las Vegas, NV
04 December 2021

36053587R00080